William Cullen Bryant

Poems collected and arranged by the author

William Cullen Bryant

Poems collected and arranged by the author

ISBN/EAN: 9783337206796

Printed in Europe, USA, Canada, Australia, Japan

Cover: Foto ©Andreas Hilbeck / pixelio.de

More available books at **www.hansebooks.com**

POEMS

BY

WILLIAM CULLEN BRYANT.

COLLECTED AND ARRANGED

BY THE AUTHOR.

NEW YORK:

D. APPLETON AND COMPANY,

846 & 848 BROADWAY.

LONDON: 16 LITTLE BRITAIN.

M.DCCC.LX.

TO THE READER.

[PREFIXED TO THE EDITION OF 1846.]

PERHAPS it would have been well if the author had followed his original intention, which was to leave out of this edition, as unworthy of republication, several of the poems which made a part of his previous collections. He asks leave to plead the judgment of a literary friend, whose opinion in such matters he highly values, as his apology for having retained them. With the exception of the first and longest poem in the collection, "The Ages," they are all arranged according to the order of time in which they were written, as far as it can be ascertained.

New York, 1846.

ADVERTISEMENT.

THE present edition has been carefully revised by the author, and some faults of diction and versification corrected. A few poems not in the previous editions have been added.

New York, August, 1854.

CONTENTS.

POEMS.

POEMS.

THE AGES.

I.

When to the common rest that crowns our days,
Called in the noon of life, the good man goes,
Or full of years, and ripe in wisdom, lays
His silver temples in their last repose;
When, o'er the buds of youth, the death-wind blows,
And blights the fairest; when our bitter tears
Stream, as the eyes of those that love us close,
We think on what they were, with many fears
Lest goodness die with them, and leave the coming
      years.

II.

And therefore, to our hearts, the days gone by,
When lived the honoured sage whose death we wept,
And the soft virtues beamed from many an eye,
And beat in many a heart that long has slept,—
Like spots of earth where angel-feet have stepped,
Are holy; and high-dreaming bards have told
Of times when worth was crowned, and faith was kept,
Ere friendship grew a snare, or love waxed cold—
Those pure and happy times—the golden days of old.

2

III.

Peace to the just man's memory; let it grow
Greener with years, and blossom through the flight
Of ages; let the mimic canvas show
His calm benevolent features; let the light
Stream on his deeds of love, that shunned the sight
Of all but heaven, and in the book of fame,
The glorious record of his virtues write,
And hold it up to men, and bid them claim
A palm like his, and catch from him the hallowed flame.

IV.

But oh, despair not of their fate who rise
To dwell upon the earth when we withdraw!
Lo! the same shaft by which the righteous dies,
Strikes through the wretch that scoffed at mercy's law
And trode his brethren down, and felt no awe
Of Him who will avenge them. Stainless worth,
Such as the sternest age of virtue saw,
Ripens, meanwhile, till time shall call it forth
From the low modest shade, to light and bless the earth.

V.

Has Nature, in her calm, majestic march
Faltered with age at last? does the bright sun
Grow dim in heaven? or, in their far blue arch,
Sparkle the crowd of stars, when day is done,
Less brightly? when the dew-lipped Spring comes on,
Breathes she with airs less soft, or scents the sky
With flowers less fair than when her reign begun?
Does prodigal Autumn, to our age, deny
The plenty that once swelled beneath his sober eye?

VI.

Look on this beautiful world, and read the truth
In her fair page; see, every season brings
New change, to her, of everlasting youth;
Still the green soil, with joyous living things,

Swarms, the wide air is full of joyous wings,
And myriads, still, are happy in the sleep
Of ocean's azure gulfs, and where he flings
The restless surge. Eternal Love doth keep
In his complacent arms, the earth, the air, the deep.

VII.

Will then the merciful One, who stamped our race
With his own image, and who gave them sway
O'er earth, and the glad dwellers on her face,
Now that our swarming nations far away
Are spread, where'er the moist earth drinks the day,
Forget the ancient care that taught and nursed
His latest offspring? will he quench the ray
Infused by his own forming smile at first,
And leave a work so fair all blighted and accursed!

VIII.

· Oh, no! a thousand cheerful omens give
Hope of yet happier days, whose dawn is nigh.
He who has tamed the elements, shall not live
The slave of his own passions; he whose eye
Unwinds the eternal dances of the sky,
And in the abyss of brightness dares to span
The sun's broad circle, rising yet more high,
In God's magnificent works his will shall scan—
And love and peace shall make their paradise with
  man.

IX.

Sit at the feet of history—through the night
Of years the steps of virtue she shall trace,
And show the earlier ages, where her sight
Can pierce the eternal shadows o'er their face;—
When, from the genial cradle of our race,
Went forth the tribes of men, their pleasant lot
To choose, where palm-groves cooled their dwelling-
  place,

Or freshening rivers ran; and there forgot
The truth of heaven, and kneeled to gods that heard
　　them not.

X.

Then waited not the murderer for the night,
But smote his brother down in the bright day,
And he who felt the wrong, and had the might,
His own avenger, girt himself to slay;
Beside the path the unburied carcass lay;
The shepherd, by the fountains of the glen,
Fled, while the robber swept his flock away,
And slew his babes.　The sick, untended then,
Languished in the damp shade, and died afar from men

XI.

But misery brought in love; in passion's strife
Man gave his heart to mercy, pleading long,
And sought out gentle deeds to gladden life;
The weak, against the sons of spoil and wrong,
Banded, and watched their hamlets, and grew strong
States rose, and, in the shadow of their might,
The timid rested.　To the reverent throng,
Grave and time-wrinkled men, with locks all white,
Gave laws, and judged their strifes, and taught the
　　way of right;

XII.

Till bolder spirits seized the rule, and nailed
On men the yoke that man should never bear,
And drove them forth to battle.　Lo! unveiled
The scene of those stern ages!　What is there!
A boundless sea of blood, and the wild air
Moans with the crimson surges that entomb
Cities and bannered armies; forms that wear
The kingly circlet rise, amid the gloom,
O'er the dark wave, and straight are swallowed in its
　　womb.

XIII.

Those ages have no memory, but they left
A record in the desert—columns strown
On the waste sands, and statues fallen and cleft,
Heaped like a host in battle overthrown;
Vast ruins, where the mountain's ribs of stone
Were hewn into a city; streets that spread
In the dark earth, where never breath has blown
Of heaven's sweet air, nor foot of man dares tread
The long and perilous ways—the Cities of the Dead:

XIV.

And tombs of monarchs to the clouds up-piled—
They perished, but the eternal tombs remain—
And the black precipice, abrupt and wild,
Pierced by long toil and hollowed to a fane;—
Huge piers and frowning forms of gods sustain
The everlasting arches, dark and wide,
Like the night-heaven, when clouds are black with rain
But idly skill was tasked, and strength was plied,
All was the work of slaves to swell a despot's pride.

XV.

And Virtue cannot dwell with slaves, nor reign
O'er those who cower to take a tyrant's yoke;
She left the down-trod nations in disdain,
And flew to Greece, when Liberty awoke,
New-born, amid those glorious vales, and broke
Sceptre and chain with her fair youthful hands:
As rocks are shivered in the thunder-stroke.
And lo! in full-grown strength, an empire stands
Of leagued and rival states, the wonder of the lands.

XVI.

Oh, Greece! thy flourishing cities were a spoil
Unto each other; thy hard hand oppressed
And crushed the helpless; thou didst make thy soil
Drunk with the blood of those that loved thee best;

And thou didst drive, from thy unnatural breast,
Thy just and brave to die in distant climes;
Earth shuddered at thy deeds, and sighed for rest
From thine abominations; after times,
That yet shall read thy tale, will tremble at thy crimes

XVII.

Yet there was that within thee which has saved
Thy glory, and redeemed thy blotted name;
The story of thy better deeds, engraved
On fame's unmouldering pillar, puts to shame
Our chiller virtue; the high art to tame
The whirlwind of the passions was thine own;
And the pure ray, that from thy bosom came,
Far over many a land and age has shone,
And mingles with the light that beams from God's own
        throne.

XVIII.

And Rome—thy sterner, younger sister, she
Who awed the world with her imperial frown—
Rome drew the spirit of her race from thee,
The rival of thy shame and thy renown.
Yet her degenerate children sold the crown
Of earth's wide kingdoms to a line of slaves;
Guilt reigned, and wo with guilt, and plagues came
        down,
Till the north broke its floodgates, and the waves
Whelmed the degraded race, and weltered o'er their
        graves.

XIX.

Vainly that ray of brightness from above,
That shone around the Galilean lake,
The light of hope, the leading star of love,
Struggled, the darkness of that day to break;
Even its own faithless guardians strove to slake,
In fogs of earth, the pure ethereal flame;
And priestly hands, for Jesus' blessed sake,

Were red with blood, and charity became,
In that stern war of forms, a mockery and a name.

XX.

They triumphed, and less bloody rites were kept
Within the quiet of the convent cell;
The well-fed inmates pattered prayer, and slept,
And sinned, and liked their easy penance well.
Where pleasant was the spot for men to dwell,
Amid its fair broad lands the abbey lay,
Sheltering dark orgies that were shame to tell,
And cowled and barefoot beggars swarmed the way,
All in their convent weeds, of black, and white, and
    gray.

XXI.

Oh, sweetly the returning muses' strain
Swelled over that famed stream, whose gentle tide
. In their bright lap the Etrurian vales detain,
Sweet, as when winter storms have ceased to chide,
And all the new-leaved woods, resounding wide,
Send out wild hymns upon the scented air.
Lo! to the smiling Arno's classic side
The emulous nations of the west repair,
And kindle their quenched urns, and drink fresh spirit
    there.

XXII.

Still, Heaven deferred the hour ordained to rend
From saintly rottenness the sacred stole;
And cowl and worshipped shrine could still defend
The wretch with felon stains upon his soul;
And crimes were set to sale, and hard his dole
Who could not bribe a passage to the skies;
And vice, beneath the mitre's kind control,
Sinned gaily on, and grew to giant size,
Shielded by priestly power, and watched by priestly
    eyes.

XXIII.

At last the earthquake came—the shock, that hurled
To dust, in many fragments dashed and strown,
The throne, whose roots were in another world,
And whose far-stretching shadow awed our own.
From many a proud monastic pile, o'erthrown,
Fear-struck, the hooded inmates rushed and fled ;
The web, that for a thousand years had grown
O'er prostrate Europe, in that day of dread
Crumbled and fell, as fire dissolves the flaxen thread.

XXIV.

The spirit of that day is still awake,
And spreads himself, and shall not sleep again ;
But through the idle mesh of power shall break
Like billows o'er the Asian monarch's chain ;
Till men are filled with him, and feel how vain,
Instead of the pure heart and innocent hands,
Are all the proud and pompous modes to gain
The smile of Heaven ;—till a new age expands
Its white and holy wings above the peaceful lands.

XXV.

For look again on the past years ;—behold,
How like the nightmare's dreams have flown away
Horrible forms of worship, that, of old,
Held, o'er the shuddering realms, unquestioned sway
See crimes, that feared not once the eye of day,
Rooted from men, without a name or place :
See nations blotted out from earth, to pay
The forfeit of deep guilt ;—with glad embrace
The fair disburdened lands welcome a nobler race.

XXVI.

Thus error's monstrous shapes from earth are driven ;
They fade, they fly—but truth survives their flight ;
Earth has no shades to quench that beam of heaven ;
Each ray that shone, in early time, to light

The faltering footstep in the path of right,
Each gleam of clearer brightness shed to aid
In man's maturer day his bolder sight,
All blended, like the rainbow's radiant braid,
Pour yet, and still shall pour, the blaze that cannot fade.

XXVII.

Late, from this western shore, that morning chased
The deep and ancient night, which threw its shroud
O'er the green land of groves, the beautiful waste,
Nurse of full streams, and lifter-up of proud
Sky-mingling mountains that o'erlook the cloud.
Erewhile, where yon gay spires their brightness rear,
Trees waved, and the brown hunter's shouts were
    loud
Amid the forest; and the bounding deer
Fled at the glancing plume, and the gaunt wolf yelled
    near.

XXVIII.

And where his willing waves yon bright blue bay
Sends up, to kiss his decorated brim,
And cradles, in his soft embrace, the gay
Young group of grassy islands born of him,
And crowding nigh, or in the distance dim,
Lifts the white throng of sails, that bear or bring
The commerce of the world;—with tawny limb,
And belt and beads in sunlight glistening,
The savage urged his skiff like wild bird on the wing

XXIX.

Then all this youthful paradise around,
And all the broad and boundless mainland, lay
Cooled by the interminable wood, that frowned
O'er mount and vale, where never summer ray
Glanced, till the strong tornado broke his way
Through the gray giants of the sylvan wild;
Yet many a sheltered glade, with blossoms gay

Beneath the showery sky and sunshine mild,
Within the shaggy arms of that dark forest smiled.

XXX.

There stood the Indian hamlet, there the lake
Spread its blue sheet that flashed with many an
    oar,
Where the brown otter plunged him from the brake,
And the deer drank: as the light gale flew o'er,
The twinkling maize-field rustled on the shore;
And while that spot, so wild, and lone, and fair,
A look of glad and guiltless beauty wore,
And peace was on the earth and in the air,
The warrior lit the pile, and bound his captive there

XXXI.

Not unavenged—the foeman, from the wood,
Beheld the deed, and when the midnight shade
Was stillest, gorged his battle-axe with blood;
All died—the wailing babe—the shrieking maid—
And in the flood of fire that scathed the glade,
The roofs went down; but deep the silence grew,
When on the dewy woods the day-beam played;
No more the cabin smokes rose wreathed and blue,
And ever, by their lake, lay moored the bark canoe.

XXXII.

Look now abroad—another race has filled
These populous borders—wide the wood recedes,
And towns shoot up, and fertile realms are tilled:
The land is full of harvests and green meads;
Streams numberless, that many a fountain feeds,
Shine, disembowered, and give to sun and breeze
Their virgin waters; the full region leads
New colonies forth, that toward the western seas
Spread, like a rapid flame among the autumnal trees.

XXXIII.

Here the free spirit of mankind, at length,
Throws its last fetters off; and who shall place
A limit to the giant's unchained strength,
Or curb his swiftness in the forward race?
On, like the comet's way through infinite space,
Stretches the long untravelled path of light,
Into the depths of ages; we may trace,
Afar, the brightening glory of its flight,
Till the receding rays are lost to human sight.

XXXIV.

Europe is given a prey to sterner fates,
And writhes in shackles; strong the arms that chain
To earth her struggling multitude of states;
She too is strong, and might not chafe in vain
Against them, but might cast to earth the train
That trample her, and break their iron net.
Yes, she shall look on brighter days and gain
The meed of worthier deeds; the moment set
To rescue and raise up, draws near—but is not yet.

XXXV.

But thou, my country, thou shalt never fall,
Save with thy children—thy maternal care,
Thy lavish love, thy blessings showered on all—
These are thy fetters—seas and stormy air
Are the wide barrier of thy borders, where,
Among thy gallant sons that guard thee well,
Thou laugh'st at enemies: who shall then declare
The date of thy deep-founded strength, or tell
How happy, in thy lap, the sons of men shall dwell?

THANATOPSIS.

To him who in the love of Nature holds
Communion with her visible forms, she speaks
A various language; for his gayer hours
She has a voice of gladness, and a smile
And eloquence of beauty, and she glides
Into his darker musings, with a mild
And healing sympathy, that steals away
Their sharpness, ere he is aware.   When thoughts
Of the last bitter hour come like a blight
Over thy spirit, and sad images
Of the stern agony, and shroud, and pall,
And breathless darkness, and the narrow house,
Make thee to shudder, and grow sick at heart;—
Go forth, under the open sky, and list
To Nature's teachings, while from all around—
Earth and her waters, and the depths of air,—
Comes a still voice—Yet a few days, and thee
The all-beholding sun shall see no more
In all his course; nor yet in the cold ground,
Where thy pale form was laid, with many tears,
Nor in the embrace of ocean, shall exist
Thy image.   Earth, that nourished thee, shall claim
Thy growth, to be resolved to earth again,
And, lost each human trace, surrendering up
Thine individual being, shalt thou go
To mix for ever with the elements,
To be a brother to the insensible rock
And to the sluggish clod, which the rude swain
Turns with his share, and treads upon.   The oak
Shall send his roots abroad, and pierce thy mould.

Yet not to thine eternal resting-place
Shalt thou retire alone, nor couldst thou wish
Couch more magnificent. Thou shalt lie down
With patriarchs of the infant world—with kings,
The powerful of the earth—the wise, the good,
Fair forms, and hoary seers of ages past,
All in one mighty sepulchre. The hills
Rock-ribbed and ancient as the sun,—the vales
Stretching in pensive quietness between ;
The venerable woods—rivers that move
In majesty, and the complaining brooks
That make the meadows green ; and, poured round all,
Old ocean's gray and melancholy waste,—
Are but the solemn decorations all
Of the great tomb of man. The golden sun,
The planets, all the infinite host of heaven,
Are shining on the sad abodes of death,
Through the still lapse of ages. All that tread
The globe are but a handful to the tribes
That slumber in its bosom.—Take the wings
Of morning, traverse Barca's desert sands,
Or lose thyself in the continuous woods
Where rolls the Oregan, and hears no sound,
Save his own dashings—yet—the dead are there :
And millions in those solitudes, since first
The flight of years began, have laid them down
In their last sleep—the dead reign there alone.
So shalt thou rest, and what if thou withdraw
In silence from the living, and no friend
Take note of thy departure ! All that breathe
Will share thy destiny. The gay will laugh
When thou art gone, the solemn brood of care
Plod on, and each one as before will chase
His favourite phantom ; yet all these shall leave
Their mirth and their employments, and shall come,
And make their bed with thee. As the long train
Of ages glide away, the sons of men,
The youth in life's green spring, and he who goes

3

In the full strength of years, matron, and maid,
And the sweet babe, and the gray-headed man,—
Shall one by one be gathered to thy side,
By those, who in their turn shall follow them.

So live, that when thy summons comes to join
The innumerable caravan, which moves
To that mysterious realm, where each shall take
His chamber in the silent halls of death,
Thou go not, like the quarry-slave at night,
Scourged to his dungeon, but, sustained and soothed
By an unfaltering trust, approach thy grave,
Like one who wraps the drapery of his couch
About him, and lies down to pleasant dreams.

THE YELLOW VIOLET.

When beechen buds begin to swell,
And woods the blue-bird's warble know,
The yellow violet's modest bell
Peeps from the last year's leaves below.

Ere russet fields their green resume,
Sweet flower, I love, in forest bare,
To meet thee, when thy faint perfume
Alone is in the virgin air.

Of all her train, the hands of Spring
First plant thee in the watery mould,
And I have seen thee blossoming
Beside the snow-bank's edges cold.

Thy parent sun, who bade thee view
 Pale skies, and chilling moisture sip,
Has bathed thee in his own bright hue,
 And streaked with jet thy glowing lip.

Yet slight thy form, and low thy seat,
 And earthward bent thy gentle eye,
Unapt the passing view to meet,
 When loftier flowers are flaunting nigh.

Oft, in the sunless April day,
 Thy early smile has stayed my walk;
But midst the gorgeous blooms of May,
 I passed thee on thy humble stalk.

So they, who climb to wealth, forget
 The friends in darker fortunes tried.
I copied them—but I regret
 That I should ape the ways of pride.

And when again the genial hour
 Awakes the painted tribes of light,
I'll not o'erlook the modest flower
 That made the woods of April bright.

———•♦•———

INSCRIPTION FOR THE ENTRANCE TO A WOOD.

Stranger, if thou hast learned a truth which needs
No school of long experience, that the world
Is full of guilt and misery, and hast seen
Enough of all its sorrows, crimes, and cares,
To tire thee of it, enter this wild wood

And view the haunts of Nature. The calm shade
Shall bring a kindred calm, and the sweet breeze
That makes the green leaves dance, shall waft a balm
To thy sick heart. Thou wilt find nothing here
Of all that pained thee in the haunts of men,
And made thee loathe thy life. The primal curse
Fell, it is true, upon the unsinning earth,
But not in vengeance. God hath yoked to guilt
Her pale tormentor, misery. Hence, these shades
Are still the abodes of gladness; the thick roof
Of green and stirring branches is alive
And musical with birds, that sing and sport
In wantonness of spirit; while below
The squirrel, with raised paws and form erect,
Chirps merrily. Throngs of insects in the shade
Try their thin wings and dance in the warm beam
That waked them into life. Even the green trees
Partake the deep contentment; as they bend
To the soft winds, the sun from the blue sky
Looks in and sheds a blessing on the scene.
Scarce less the cleft-born wild-flower seems to enjoy
Existence, than the winged plunderer
That sucks its sweets. The mossy rocks themselves,
And the old and ponderous trunks of prostrate trees
That lead from knoll to knoll a causey rude
Or bridge the sunken brook, and their dark roots,
With all their earth upon them, twisting high,
Breathe fixed tranquillity. The rivulet
Sends forth glad sounds, and tripping o'er its bed
Of pebbly sands, or leaping down the rocks,
Seems, with continuous laughter, to rejoice
In its own being. Softly tread the marge,
Lest from her midway perch thou scare the wren
That dips her bill in water. The cool wind,
That stirs the stream in play, shall come to thee,
Like one that loves thee nor will let thee pass
Ungreeted, and shall give its light embrace.

SONG.

Soon as the glazed and gleaming snow
   Reflects the day-dawn cold and clear,
The hunter of the west must go
   In depth of woods to seek the deer.

His rifle on his shoulder placed,
   His stores of death arranged with skill,
His moccasins and snow-shoes laced,—
   Why lingers he beside the hill?

Far, in the dim and doubtful light,
   Where woody slopes a valley leave,
He sees what none but lover might,
   The dwelling of his Genevieve.

And oft he turns his truant eye,
   And pauses oft, and lingers near;
But when he marks the reddening sky,
   He bounds away to hunt the deer.

TO A WATERFOWL.

Whither, midst falling dew,
While glow the heavens with the last steps of day,
Far, through their rosy depths, dost thou persue
   Thy solitary way?

Vainly the fowler's eye
Might mark thy distant flight to do thee wrong,
As, darkly limned upon the crimson sky,
Thy figure floats along.

Seek'st thou the plashy brink
Of weedy lake, or marge of river wide,
Or where the rocking billows rise and sink
On the chafed ocean side !

There is a Power whose care
Teaches thy way along that pathless coast,—
The desert and illimitable air,—
Lone wandering, but not lost.

All day thy wings have fanned,
At that far height, the cold, thin atmosphere,
Yet stoop not, weary, to the welcome land,
Though the dark night is near.

And soon that toil shall end ;
Soon shalt thou find a summer home, and rest,
And scream among thy fellows ; reeds shall bend,
Soon, o'er thy sheltered nest.

Thou'rt gone, the abyss of heaven
Hath swallowed up thy form ; yet, on my heart
Deeply hath sunk the lesson thou hast given,
And shall not soon depart.

He who, from zone to zone,
Guides through the boundless sky thy certain flight,
In the long way that I must tread alone,
Will lead my steps aright.

GREEN RIVER.

WHEN breezes are soft and skies are fair,
I steal an hour from study and care,
And hie me away to the woodland scene,
Where wanders the stream with waters of green,
As if the bright fringe of herbs on its brink
Had given their stain to the wave they drink;
And they, whose meadows it murmurs through,
Have named the stream from its own fair hue.

Yet pure its waters—its shallows are bright
With coloured pebbles and sparkles of light,
And clear the depths where its eddies play,
And dimples deepen and whirl away,
And the plane-tree's speckled arms o'ershoot
The swifter current that mines its root,
Through whose shifting leaves, as you walk the hill,
The quivering glimmer of sun and rill
With a sudden flash on the eye is thrown,
Like the ray that streams from the diamond-stone.
Oh, loveliest there the spring days come,
With blossoms, and birds, and wild bees' hum;
The flowers of summer are fairest there,
And freshest the breath of the summer air;
And sweetest the golden autumn day
In silence and sunshine glides away.

Yet fair as thou art, thou shunnest to glide,
Beautiful stream! by the village side;
But windest away from haunts of men,
To quiet valley and shaded glen;
And forest, and meadow, and slope of hill,
Around thee, are lonely, lovely, and still.

Lonely—save when, by thy rippling tides,
From thicket to thicket the angler glides;
Or the simpler comes, with basket and book, '
For herbs of power on thy banks to look;
Or haply, some idle dreamer, like me,
To wander, and muse, and gaze on thee.
Still—save the chirp of birds that feed
On the river cherry and seedy reed,
And thy own wild music gushing out
With mellow murmur or fairy shout,
From dawn to the blush of another day,
Like traveller singing along his way.

That fairy music I never hear,
Nor gaze on those waters so green and clear,
And mark them winding away from sight,
Darkened with shade or flashing with light,
While o'er them the vine to its thicket clings,
And the zephyr stoops to freshen his wings,
But I wish that fate had left me free
To wander these quiet haunts with thee,
Till the eating cares of earth should depart,
And the peace of the scene pass into my heart;
And I envy thy stream, as its glides along,
Through its beautiful banks in a trance of song.

Though forced to drudge for the dregs of men,
And scrawl strange words with the barbarous pen,
And mingle among the jostling crowd,
Where the sons of strife are subtle and loud—
I often come to this quiet place,
To breathe the airs that ruffle thy face,
And gaze upon thee in silent dream,
For in thy lonely and lovely stream
An image of that calm life appears
That won my heart in my greener years.

.

A WINTER PIECE.

THE time has been that these wild solitudes,
Yet beautiful as wild, were trod by me
Oftener than now ; and when the ills of life
Had chafed my spirit—when the unsteady pulse
Beat with strange flutterings—I would wander forth
And seek the woods. The sunshine on my path
Was to me as a friend. The swelling hills,
The quiet dells retiring far between,
With gentle invitation to explore
Their windings, were a calm society
That talked with me and soothed me. Then the chant
Of birds, and chime of brooks, and soft caress
.Of the fresh sylvan air, made me forget
The thoughts that broke my peace, and I began
To gather simples by the fountain's brink,
And lose myself in day-dreams. While I stood
In nature's loneliness, I was with one
With whom I early grew familiar, one
Who never had a frown for me, whose voice
Never rebuked me for the hours I stole
From cares I loved not, but of which the world
Deems highest, to converse with her. When shrieked
The bleak November winds, and smote the woods,
And the brown fields were herbless, and the shades,
That met above the merry rivulet,
Were spoiled, I sought, I loved them still; they seemed
Like old companions in adversity.
Still there was beauty in my walks; the brook,
Bordered with sparkling frost-work, was as gay
As with its fringe of summer flowers. Afar,
The village with its spires, the path of streams

And dim receding valleys, hid before
By interposing trees, lay visible
Through the bare grove, and my familiar haunts
Seemed new to me. Nor was I slow to come
Among them, when the clouds, from their still skirts,
Had shaken down on earth the feathery snow,
And all was white. The pure keen air abroad,
Albeit it breathed no scent of herb, nor heard
Love-call of bird nor merry hum of bee,
Was not the air of death. Bright mosses crept
Over the spotted trunks, and the close buds,
That lay along the boughs, instinct with life,
Patient, and waiting the soft breath of Spring,
Feared not the piercing spirit of the North.
The snow-bird twittered on the beechen bough,
And 'neath the hemlock, whose thick branches bent
Beneath its bright cold burden, and kept dry
A circle, on the earth, of withered leaves,
The partridge found a shelter. Through the snow
The rabbit sprang away. The lighter track
Of fox, and the racoon's broad path, were there,
Crossing each other. From his hollow tree,
The squirrel was abroad, gathering the nuts
Just fallen, that asked the winter cold and sway
Of winter blast, to shake them from their hold.

But Winter has yet brighter scenes,—he boasts
Splendors beyond what gorgeous Summer knows;
Or Autumn with his many fruits, and woods
All flushed with many hues. Come when the rains
Have glazed the snow, and clothed the trees with ice
While the slant sun of February pours
Into the bowers a flood of light. Approach!
The incrusted surface shall upbear thy steps,
And the broad arching portals of the grove
Welcome thy entering. Look! the massy trunks
Are cased in the pure crystal; each light spray,
Nodding and tinkling in the breath of heaven,

Is studded with its trembling water-drops,
That glimmer with an amethystine light.
But round the parent stem the long low boughs
Bend, in a glittering ring, and arbors hide
The glassy floor. Oh! you might deem the spot
The spacious cavern of some virgin mine,
Deep in the womb of earth—where the gems grow,
And diamonds put forth radiant rods and bud
With amethyst and topaz—and the place
Lit up, most royally, with the pure beam
That dwells in them. Or haply the vast hall
Of fairy palace, that outlasts the night,
And fades not in the glory of the sun ;—
Where crystal columns send forth slender shafts
And crossing arches; and fantastic aisles
Wind from the sight in brightness, and are lost
Among the crowded pillars. Raise thine eye;
Thou seest no cavern roof, no palace vault;
There the blue sky and the white drifting cloud
Look in. Again the wildered fancy dreams
Of spouting fountains, frozen as they rose,
And fixed, with all their branching jets, in air,
And all their sluices sealed. All, all is light;
Light without shade. But all shall pass away
With the next sun. From numberless vast trunks,
Loosened, the crashing ice shall make a sound
Like the far roar of rivers, and the eve
Shall close o'er the brown woods as it was wont.

And it is pleasant, when the noisy streams
Are just set free, and milder suns melt off
The plashy snow, save only the firm drift
In the deep glen or the close shade of pines,—
'Tis pleasant to behold the wreaths of smoke
Roll up among the maples of the hill,
Where the shrill sound of youthful voices wakes
The shriller echo, as the clear pure lymph,
That from the wounded trees, in twinkling drops,

Falls, mid the golden brightness of the morn,
Is gathered in with brimming pails, and oft,
Wielded by sturdy hands, the stroke of axe
Makes the woods ring. Along the quiet air,
Come and float calmly off the soft light clouds,
Such as you see in summer, and the winds
Scarce stir the branches. Lodged in sunny cleft,
Where the cold breezes come not, blooms alone
The little wind-flower, whose just opened eye
Is blue as the spring heaven it gazes at—
Startling the loiterer in the naked groves
With unexpected beauty, for the time
Of blossoms and green leaves is yet afar.
And ere it comes, the encountering winds shall oft
Muster their wrath again, and rapid clouds
Shade heaven, and bounding on the frozen earth
Shall fall their volleyed stores, rounded like hail
And white like snow, and the loud North again
Shall buffet the vexed forest in his rage.

THE WEST WIND.

Beneath the forest's skirt I rest,
  Whose branching pines rise dark and high,
And hear the breezes of the West
  Among the thread-like foliage sigh.

Sweet Zephyr! why that sound of woe?
  Is not thy home among the flowers?
Do not the bright June roses blow,
  To meet thy kiss at morning hours?

And lo! thy glorious realm outspread—
  Yon stretching valleys, green and gay,
And yon free hill-tops, o'er whose head
  The loose white clouds are borne away.

And there the full broad river runs,
  And many a fount wells fresh and sweet,
To cool thee when the mid-day suns
  Have made thee faint beneath their heat.

Thou wind of joy, and youth, and love;
  Spirit of the new-wakened year!
The sun in his blue realm above
  Smooths a bright path when thou art here.

In lawns the murmuring bee is heard,
  The wooing ring-dove in the shade;
On thy soft breath, the new-fledged bird
  Takes wing, half happy, half afraid.

Ah! thou art like our wayward race;—
  When not a shade of pain or ill
Dims the bright smile of Nature's face,
  Thou lov'st to sigh and murmur still.

THE BURIAL-PLACE.

A FRAGMENT.

EREWHILE, on England's pleasant shores, our sires
Left not their churchyards unadorned with shades
Or blossoms, but indulgent to the strong
And natural dread of man's last home, the grave,
Its frost and silence—they disposed around,

4

To soothe the melancholy spirit that dwelt
Too sadly on life's close, the forms and hues
Of vegetable beauty.　There the yew,
Green even amid the snows of winter, told
Of immortality, and gracefully
The willow, a perpetual mourner, drooped;
And there the gadding woodbine crept about,
And there the ancient ivy.　From the spot
Where the sweet maiden, in her blossoming years
Cut off, was laid with streaming eyes, and hands
That trembled as they placed her there, the rose
Sprung modest, on bowed stalk, and better spoke
Her graces, than the proudest monument.
There children set about their playmate's grave
The pansy.　On the infant's little bed,
Wet at its planting with maternal tears,
Emblem of early sweetness, early death,
Nestled the lowly primrose.　Childless dames,
And maids that would not raise the reddened eye—
Orphans, from whose young lids the light of joy
Fled early,—silent lovers, who had given
All that they lived for to the arms of earth,
Came often, o'er the recent graves to strew
Their offerings, rue, and rosemary, and flowers.

　　The pilgrim bands who passed the sea to keep
Their Sabbaths in the eye of God alone,
In his wide temple of the wilderness,
Brought not these simple customs of the heart
With them.　It might be, while they laid their dead
By the vast solemn skirts of the old groves,
And the fresh virgin soil poured forth strange flowers
About their graves; and the familiar shades
Of their own native isle, and wonted blooms,
And herbs were wanting, which the pious hand
Might plant or scatter there, these gentle rites
Passed out of use.　Now they are scarcely known,
And rarely in our borders may you meet

The tall larch, sighing in the burial-place,
Or willow, trailing low its boughs to hide
The gleaming marble.   Naked rows of graves
And melancholy ranks of monuments
Are seen instead, where the coarse grass, between,
Shoots up its dull green spikes, and in the wind
Hisses, and the neglected bramble nigh,
Offers its berries to the schoolboy's hand,
In vain—they grow too near the dead.   Yet here,
Nature, rebuking the neglect of man,
Plants often, by the ancient mossy stone,
The brier rose, and upon the broken turf
That clothes the fresher grave, the strawberry plant
Sprinkles its swell with blossoms, and lays forth
Her ruddy, pouting fruit.   *   *   *   *   *

"BLESSED ARE THEY THAT MOURN."

Oh, deem not they are blest alone
   Whose lives a peaceful tenor keep;
The Power who pities man, has shown
   A blessing for the eyes that weep.

The light of smiles shall fill again
   The lids that overflow with tears;
And weary hours of woe and pain
   Are promises of happier years.

There is a day of sunny rest
   For every dark and troubled night;
And grief may bide an evening guest,
   But joy shall come with early light.

And thou, who, o'er thy friend's low bier,
  Sheddest the bitter drops like rain,
Hope that a brighter, happier sphere
  Will give him to thy arms again.

Nor let the good man's trust depart,
  Though life its common gifts deny,—
Though with a pierced and bleeding heart
  And spurned of men, he goes to die.

For God hath marked each sorrowing day
  And numbered every secret tear,
And heaven's long age of bliss shall pay
  For all his children suffer here.

'NO MAN KNOWETH HIS SEPULCHRE."

WHEN he, who, from the scourge of wrong,
  Aroused the Hebrew tribes to fly,
Saw the fair region, promised long,
  And bowed him on the hills to die;

God made his grave, to men unknown,
  Where Moab's rocks a vale infold,
And laid the aged seer alone
  To slumber while the world grows old.

Thus still, whene'er the good and just
  Close the dim eye on life and pain,
Heaven watches o'er their sleeping dust
  Till the pure spirit comes again.

Though nameless, trampled, and forgot,
  His servant's humble ashes lie,
Yet God has marked and sealed the spot,
  To call its inmate to the sky.

A WALK AT SUNSET.

WHEN insect wings are glistening in the beam
  Of the low sun, and mountain-tops are bright,
Oh, let me, by the crystal valley-stream,
  Wander amid the mild and mellow light;
And while the wood-thrush pipes his evening lay,
Give me one lonely hour to hymn the setting day.

Oh, sun! that o'er the western mountains now
  Go'st down in glory! ever beautiful
And blessed is thy radiance, whether thou
  Colorest the eastern heaven and night-mist cool,
Till the bright day-star vanish, or on high
Climbest and streamest thy white splendors from mid-
    sky.

Yet, loveliest are thy setting smiles, and fair,
  Fairest of all that earth beholds, the hues
That live among the clouds, and flush the air,
  Lingering and deepening at the hour of dews.
Then softest gales are breathed, and softest heard
The plaining voice of streams, and pensive note of
    bird.

They who here roamed, of yore, the forest wide,
  Felt, by such charm, their simple bosoms won;
They deemed their quivered warrior, when he died,
  Went to bright isles beneath the setting sun;

Where winds are aye at peace, and skies are fair,
And purple-skirted clouds curtain the crimson air.

So, with the glories of the dying day,
    Its thousand trembling lights and changing hues,
The memory of the brave who passed away
    Tenderly mingled;—fitting hour to muse
On such grave theme, and sweet the dream that shed
Brightness and beauty round the destiny of the dead.

For ages, on the silent forests here,
    Thy beams did fall before the red man came
To dwell beneath them; in their shade the deer
    Fed, and feared not the arrow's deadly aim.
Nor tree was felled, in all that world of woods,
Save by the beaver's tooth, or winds, or rush of floods.

Then came the hunter tribes, and thou didst look,
  . For ages, on their deeds in the hard chase,
And well-fought wars; green sod and silver brook
    Took the first stain of blood; before thy face
The warrior generations came and passed,
And glory was laid up for many an age to last.

Now they are gone, gone as thy setting blaze
    Goes down the west, while night is pressing on,
And with them the old tale of better days,
    And trophies of remembered power, are gone.
Yon field that gives the harvest, where the plough
Strikes the white bone, is all that tells their story now.

I stand upon their ashes in thy beam,
    The offspring of another race, I stand,
Beside a stream they loved, this valley stream;
    And where the night-fire of the quivered band
Showed the gray oak by fits, and war-song rung,
I teach the quiet shades the strains of this new tongue.

Farewell! but thou shalt come again—thy light
    Must shine on other changes, and behold
The place of the thronged city still as night—
    States fallen—new empires built upon the old—
But never shalt thou see these realms again
Darkened by boundless groves, and roamed by savage
    men.

HYMN TO DEATH.

Oh! could I hope the wise and pure in heart
Might hear my song without a frown, nor deem
My voice unworthy of the theme it tries,—
I would take up the hymn to Death, and say
To the grim power, The world hath slandered thee
And mocked thee. On thy dim and shadowy brow
They place an iron crown, and call thee king
Of terrors, and the spoiler of the world,
Deadly assassin, that strik'st down the fair,
The loved, the good—that breathest on the lights
Of virtue set along the vale of life,
And they go out in darkness. I am come,
Not with reproaches, not with cries and prayers,
Such as have stormed thy stern, insensible ear
From the beginning; I am come to speak
Thy praises. True it is, that I have wept
Thy conquests, and may weep them yet again
And thou from some I love wilt take a life
Dear to me as my own. Yet while the spell
Is on my spirit, and I talk with thee
In sight of all thy trophies, face to face,
Meet is it that my voice should utter forth
Thy nobler triumphs; I will teach the world

To thank thee. Who are thine accusers?—Who?
The living!—they who never felt thy power,
And know thee not. The curses of the wretch
Whose crimes are ripe, his sufferings when thy hand
Is on him, and the hour he dreads is come,
Are writ among thy praises. But the good—
Does he whom thy kind hand dismissed to peace,
Upbraid the gentle violence that took off
His fetters, and unbarred his prison cell?

    Raise then the hymn to Death. Deliverer!
God hath anointed thee to free the oppressed
And crush the oppressor. When the armed chief,
The conqueror of nations, walks the world,
And it is changed beneath his feet, and all
Its kingdoms melt into one mighty realm—
Thou, while his head is loftiest and his heart
Blasphemes, imagining his own right hand
Almighty, thou dost set thy sudden grasp
Upon him, and the links of that strong chain
Which bound mankind are crumbled; thou dost break
Sceptre and crown, and beat his throne to dust.
Then the earth shouts with gladness, and her tribes
Gather within their ancient bounds again.
Else had the mighty of the olden time,
Nimrod, Sesostris, or the youth who feigned
His birth from Libyan Ammon, smitten yet
The nations with a rod of iron, and driven
Their chariot o'er our necks. Thou dost avenge,
In thy good time, the wrongs of those who know
No other friend. Nor dost thou interpose
Only to lay the sufferer asleep,
Where he who made him wretched troubles not
His rest—thou dost strike down his tyrant too.
Oh, there is joy when hands that held the scourge
Drop lifeless, and the pitiless heart is cold.
Thou too dost purge from earth its horrible
And old idolatries;—from the proud fanes

Each to his grave their priests go out, till none
Is left to teach their worship; then the fires
Of sacrifice are chilled, and the green moss
O'ercreeps their altars; the fallen images
Cumber the weedy courts, and for loud hymns,
Chanted by kneeling multitudes, the wind
Shrieks in the solitary aisles. When he
Who gives his life to guilt, and laughs at all
The laws that God or man has made, and round
Hedges his seat with power, and shines in wealth,—
Lifts up his atheist front to scoff at Heaven,
And celebrates his shame in open day,
Thou, in the pride of all his crimes, cutt'st off
The horrible example. Touched by thine,
The extortioner's hard hand foregoes the gold
Wrung from the o'er-worn poor. The perjurer,
Whose tongue was lithe, e'en now, and voluble
Against his neighbor's life, and he who laughed
And leaped for joy to see a spotless fame
Blasted before his own foul calumnies,
Are smit with deadly silence. He, who sold
His conscience to preserve a worthless life,
Even while he hugs himself on his escape,
Trembles, as, doubly terrible, at length,
Thy steps o'ertake him, and there is no time
For parley, nor will bribes unclench thy grasp.
Oft, too, dost thou reform thy victim, long
Ere his last hour. And when the reveller,
Mad in the chase of pleasure, stretches on,
And strains each nerve, and clears the path of life
Like wind, thou point'st him to the dreadful goal,
And shak'st thy hour-glass in his reeling eye,
And check'st him in mid course. Thy skeleton hand
Shows to the faint of spirit the right path,
And he is warned, and fears to step aside.
Thou sett'st between the ruffian and his crime
Thy ghastly countenance, and his slack hand
Drops the drawn knife. But, oh, most fearfully

Dost thou show forth Heaven's justice, when thy shafts
Drink up the ebbing spirit—then the hard
Of heart and violent of hand restores
The treasure to the friendless wretch ho wronged.
Then from the writhing bosom thou dost pluck
The guilty secret; lips, for ages sealed,
Are faithless to their dreadful trust at length,
And give it up; the felon's latest breath
Absolves the innocent man who bears his crime;
The slanderer, horror-smitten, and in tears,
Recalls the deadly obloquy he forged
To work his brother's ruin.   Thou dost make
Thy penitent victim utter to the air
The dark conspiracy that strikes at life,
And aims to whelm the laws; ere yet the hour
Is come, and the dread sign of murder given.

Thus, from the first of time, hast thou been found
On virtue's side; the wicked, but for thee,
Had been too strong for the good; the great of earth
Had crushed the weak for ever.   Schooled in guile
For ages, while each passing year had brought
Its baneful lesson, they had filled the world
With their abominations; while its tribes,
Trodden to earth, imbruted, and despoiled,
Had knelt to them in worship; sacrifice
Had smoked on many an altar, temple roofs
Had echoed with the blasphemous prayer and hymn:
But thou, the great reformer of the world,
Tak'st off the sons of violence and fraud
In their green pupilage, their lore half learned—
Ere guilt had quite o'errun the simple heart
God gave them at their birth, and blotted out
His image.   Thou dost mark them flushed with hope,
As on the threshold of their vast designs
Doubtful and loose they stand, and strik'st them
      down.
    *   *   *   *   *

Alas! I little thought that the stern power
Whose fearful praise I sung, would try me thus
Before the strain was ended. It must cease—
For he is in his grave who taught my youth
The art of verse, and in the bud of life
Offered me to the muses. Oh, cut off
Untimely! when thy reason in its strength,
Ripened by years of toil and studious search,
And watch of Nature's silent lessons, taught
Thy hand to practise best the lenient art
To which thou gavest thy laborious days,
And, last, thy life. And, therefore, when the earth
Received thee, tears were in unyielding eyes
And on hard cheeks, and they who deemed thy skill
Delayed their death-hour, shuddered and turned pale
When thou wert gone. This faltering verse, which thou
Shalt not, as wont, o'erlook, is all I have
To offer at thy grave—this—and the hope
To copy thy example, and to leave
A name of which the wretched shall not think
As of an enemy's, whom they forgive
As all forgive the dead. Rest, therefore, thou
Whose early guidance trained my infant steps—
Rest, in the bosom of God, till the brief sleep
Of death is over, and a happier life
Shall dawn to waken thine insensible dust.

Now thou art not—and yet the men whose guilt
Has wearied Heaven for vengeance—he who bears
False witness—he who takes the orphan's bread,
And robs the widow—he who spreads abroad
Polluted hands in mockery of prayer,
Are left to cumber earth. Shuddering I look
On what is written, yet I blot not out
The desultory numbers; let them stand,
The record of an idle revery.

THE MASSACRE AT SCIO.

WEEP not for Scio's children slain;
   Their blood, by Turkish falchions shed,
Sends not its cry to Heaven in vain
   For vengeance on the murderer's head.

Though high the warm red torrent ran
   Between the flames that lit the sky,
Yet, for each drop, an armed man
   Shall rise, to free the land, or die.

And for each corpse, that in the sea
   Was thrown, to feast the scaly herds,
A hundred of the foe shall be
   A banquet for the mountain birds.

Stern rites and sad, shall Greece ordain
   To keep that day, along her shore,
Till the last link of slavery's chain
   Is shivered, to be worn no more.

———•••———

THE INDIAN GIRL'S LAMENT.

AN Indian girl was sitting where
   Her lover, slain in battle, slept;
Her maiden veil, her own black hair,
   Came down o'er eyes that wept;
And wildly, in her woodland tongue,
This sad and simple lay she sung:

" I've pulled away the shrubs that grew
    Too close above thy sleeping head,
And broke the forest boughs that threw
    Their shadows o'er thy bed,
That, shining from the sweet southwest,
The sunbeams might rejoice thy rest.

" It was a weary, weary road
    That led thee to the pleasant coast,
Where thou, in his serene abcde,
    Hast met thy father's ghost ;
Where everlasting autumn lies
On yellow woods and sunny skies.

" 'Twas I the broidered mocsen made,
    That shod thee for that distant land ;
'Twas I thy bow and arrows laid
    Beside thy still cold hand ;
Thy bow in many a battle bent,
Thy arrows never vainly sent.

" With wampum belts I crossed thy breast,
    And wrapped thee in the bison's hide,
And laid the food that pleased thee best,
    In plenty, by thy side,
And decked thee bravely, as became
A warrior of illustrious name.

" Thou'rt happy now, for thou hast passed
    The long dark journey of the grave,
And in the land of light, at last,
    Hast joined the good and brave ;
Amid the flushed and balmy air,
The bravest and the loveliest there.

" Yet, oft to thine own Indian maid
    Even there thy thoughts will earthward stray,—
To her who sits where thou wert laid,
    And weeps the hours away,

Yet almost can her grief forget,
To think that thou dost love her yet.

"And thou, by one of those still lakes
   That in a shining cluster lie,
On which the south wind scarcely breaks
   The image of the sky,
A bower for thee and me hast made
Beneath the many-colored shade.

" And thou dost wait and watch to meet
   My spirit sent to join the blessed,
And, wondering what detains my feet
   From the bright land of rest,
Dost seem, in every sound, to hear
The rustling of my footsteps near."

ODE FOR AN AGRICULTURAL CELEBRATION

FAR back in the ages,
   The plough with wreaths was crowned;
The hands of kings and sages
   Entwined the chaplet round;
Till men of spoil disdained the toil
   By which the world was nourished,
And dews of blood enriched the soil
   Where green their laurels flourished:
—Now the world her fault repairs—
   The guilt that stains her story;
And weeps her crimes amid the cares
   That formed her earliest glory.

The proud throne shall crumble,
　The diadem shall wane,
The tribes of earth shall humble
　The pride of those who reign;
And War shall lay his pomp away;—
　The fame that heroes cherish,
The glory earned in deadly fray
　Shall fade, decay, and perish.
Honor waits, o'er all the Earth,
　Through endless generations,
The art that calls her harvests forth,
　And feeds the expectant nations.

------ ◆◆◆ ------

RIZPAH.

And he delivered them into the hands of the Gibeonites, and they hanged them in the hill before the Lord; and they fell all seven together, and were put to death in the days of the harvest, in the first days, in the beginning of barley-harvest.

And Rizpah, the daughter of Aiah, took sackcloth, and spread it for her upon the rock, from the beginning of harvest until the water dropped upon them out of heaven, and suffered neither the birds of the air to rest upon them by day, nor the beasts of the field by night. 　2 SAMUEL, xxi. 10.

HEAR what the desolate Rizpah said,
As on Gibeah's rocks she watched the dead.
The sons of Michal before her lay,
And her own fair children, dearer than they:
By a death of shame they all had died,
And were stretched on the bare rock, side by side.
And Rizpah, once the loveliest of all
That bloomed and smiled in the court of Saul,
All wasted with watching and famine now,
And scorched by the sun her haggard brow,
Sat mournfully guarding their corpses there,
And murmured a strange and solemn air;
The low, heart-broken, and wailing strain
Of a mother that mourns her children slain:

"I have made the crags my home, and spread
On their desert backs my sackcloth bed;
I have eaten the bitter herb of the rocks,
And drunk the midnight dew in my locks;
I have wept till I could not weep, and the pain
Of my burning eyeballs went to my brain.
Seven blackened corpses before me lie,
In the blaze of the sun and the winds of the sky.
I have watched them through the burning day,
And driven the vulture and raven away;
And the cormorant wheeled in circles round,
Yet feared to alight on the guarded ground.
And when the shadows of twilight came,
I have seen the hyena's eyes of flame,
And heard at my side his stealthy tread,
But aye at my shout the savage fled:
And I threw the lighted brand to fright
The jackal and wolf that yelled in the night.

"Ye were foully murdered, my hapless sons,
By the hands of wicked and cruel ones;
Ye fell, in your fresh and blooming prime,
All innocent, for your father's crime.
He sinned—but he paid the price of his guilt
When his blood by a nameless hand was spilt;
When he strove with the heathen host in vain,
And fell with the flower of his people slain,
And the sceptre his children's hands should sway
From his injured lineage passed away.

"But I hoped that the cottage roof would be
A safe retreat for my sons and me;
And that while they ripened to manhood fast,
They should wean my thoughts from the woes of the past.
And my bosom swelled with a mother's pride,
As they stood in their beauty and strength by my side,
Tall like their sire, with the princely grace
Of his stately form, and the bloom of his face.

"Oh, what an hour for a mother's heart,
When the pitiless ruffians tore us apart!
When I clasped their knees and wept and prayed,
And struggled and shrieked to Heaven for aid,
And clung to my sons with desperate strength,
Till the murderers loosed my hold at length,
And bore me breathless and faint aside,
In their iron arms, while my children died.
They died—and the mother that gave them birth
Is forbid to cover their bones with earth.

"The barley-harvest was nodding white,
When my children died on the rocky height,
And the reapers were singing on hill and plain,
When I came to my task of sorrow and pain.
But now the season of rain is nigh,
The sun is dim in the thickening sky,
And the clouds in sullen darkness rest
Where he hides his light at the doors of the west.
· I hear the howl of the wind that brings
The long drear storm on its heavy wings;
But the howling wind and the driving rain
Will beat on my houseless head in vain:
I shall stay, from my murdered sons to scare
The beasts of the desert, and fowls of air."

———————◆◆◆———————

THE OLD MAN'S FUNERAL.

I saw an aged man upon his bier,
   His hair was thin and white, and on his brow
A record of the cares of many a year;—
   Cares that were ended and forgotten now.
And there was sadness round, and faces bowed,
And woman's tears fell fast, and children wailed aloud.

Then rose another hoary man and said,
   In faltering accents, to that weeping train,
"Why mourn ye that our aged friend is dead?
   Ye are not sad to see the gathered grain,
Nor when their mellow fruit the orchards cast,
Nor when the yellow woods let fall the ripened
    mast.

"Ye sigh not when the sun, his course fulfilled,
   His glorious course, rejoicing earth and sky,
In the soft evening, when the winds are stilled,
   Sinks where his islands of refreshment lie,
And leaves the smile of his departure, spread
O'er the warm-colored heaven and ruddy mountain
    head.

"Why weep ye then for him, who, having won
   The bound of man's appointed years, at last,
Life's blessings all enjoyed, life's labors done,
   Serenely to his final rest has passed;
While the soft memory of his virtues, yet,
Lingers like twilight hues, when the bright sun is
    set?

"His youth was innocent; his riper age
   Marked with some act of goodness every day;
And watched by eyes that loved him, calm, and sage,
   Faded his late declining years away.
Cheerful he gave his being up, and went
To share the holy rest that waits a life well spent.

"That life was happy; every day he gave
   Thanks for the fair existence that was his;
For a sick fancy made him not her slave,
   To mock him with her phantom miseries.
No chronic tortures racked his aged limb,
For luxury and sloth had nourished none for him.

" And I am glad that he has lived thus long,
 And glad that he has gone to his reward;
Nor can I deem that nature did him wrong,
 Softly to disengage the vital cord.
For when his hand grew palsied, and his eye
Dark with the mists of age, it was his time to die."

THE RIVULET.

THIS little rill, that from the springs
Of yonder grove its current brings,
Plays on the slope awhile, and then
Goes prattling into groves again,
Oft to its warbling waters drew
My little feet, when life was new.
When woods in early green were dressed,
And from the chambers of the west
The warmer breezes, travelling out,
Breathed the new scent of flowers about,
My truant steps from home would stray,
Upon its grassy side to play,
List the brown thrasher's vernal hymn,
And crop the violet on its brim,
With blooming cheek and open brow,
As young and gay, sweet rill, as thou.

And when the days of boyhood came,
And I had grown in love with fame,
Duly I sought thy banks, and tried
My first rude numbers by thy side.
Words cannot tell how bright and gay
The scenes of life before me lay.

Then glorious hopes, that now to speak
Would bring the blood into my cheek,
Passed o'er me; and I wrote, on high,
A name I deemed should never die.

Years change thee not.   Upon yon hill
The tall old maples, verdant still,
Yet tell, in grandeur of decay,
How swift the years have passed away,
Since first, a child, and half afraid,
I wandered in the forest shade.
Thou, ever joyous rivulet,
Dost dimple, leap, and prattle yet;
And sporting with the sands that pave
The windings of thy silver wave,
And dancing to thy own wild chime,
Thou laughest at the lapse of time.
The same sweet sounds are in my ear
My early childhood loved to hear;
As pure thy limpid waters run;
As bright they sparkle to the sun;
As fresh and thick the bending ranks
Of herbs that line thy oozy banks;
The violet there, in soft May dew,
Comes up, as modest and as blue;
As green amid thy current's stress,
Floats the scarce-rooted watercress:
And the brown ground-bird, in thy glen,
Still chirps as merrily as then.

Thou changest not—but I am changed
Since first thy pleasant banks I ranged;
And the grave stranger, come to see
The play-place of his infancy,
Has scarce a single trace of him
Who sported once upon thy brim.
The visions of my youth are past—
Too bright, too beautiful to last.

I've tried the world—it wears no more
The coloring of romance it wore.
Yet well has Nature kept the truth
She promised in my earliest youth.
The radiant beauty shed abroad ·
On all the glorious works of God,
Shows freshly, to my sobered eye,
Each charm it wore in days gone by.

A few brief years shall pass away,
And I, all trembling, weak, and gray,
Bowed to the earth, which waits to fold
My ashes in the embracing mould,
(If haply the dark will of fate
Indulge my life so long a date),
May come for the last time to look
Upon my childhood's favorite brook.
Then dimly on my eye shall gleam
The sparkle of thy dancing stream;
And faintly on my ear shall fall
Thy prattling current's merry call;
Yet shalt thou flow as glad and bright
As when thou met'st my infant sight.

And I shall sleep—and on thy side,
As ages after ages glide,
Children their early sports shall try,
And pass to hoary age and die.
But thou, unchanged from year to year,
Gayly shalt play and glitter here;
Amid young flowers and tender grass
Thy endless infancy shalt pass;
And, singing down thy narrow glen,
Shalt mock the fading race of men.

MARCH

THE stormy March is come at last
   With wind, and cloud, and changing skies;
I hear the rushing of the blast,
   That through the snowy valley flies.

Ah, passing few are they who speak,
   Wild stormy month! in praise of thee;
Yet, though thy winds are loud and bleak,
   Thou art a welcome month to me.

For thou, to northern lands, again
   The glad and glorious sun dost bring,
And thou hast joined the gentle train
   And wear'st the gentle name of Spring.

And, in thy reign of blast and storm,
   Smiles many a long, bright, sunny day,
When the changed winds are soft and warm,
   And heaven puts on the blue of May.

Then sing aloud the gushing rills
   From winter's durance just set free,
And, brightly leaping down the hills,
   Begin their journey to the sea.

The year's departing beauty hides
   Of wintry storms the sullen threat;
But in thy sternest frown abides
   A look of kindly promise yet.

Thou bring'st the hope of those calm skies,
And that soft time of sunny showers,
When the wide bloom, on earth that lies,
Seems of a brighter world than ours.

———————•••———————

CONSUMPTION.

Ay, thou art for the grave; thy glances shine
Too brightly to shine long; another Spring
Shall deck her for men's eyes,—but not for thine—
Sealed in a sleep which knows no wakening.
The fields for thee have no medicinal leaf,
And the vexed ore no mineral of power;
And they who love thee wait in anxious grief
Till the slow plague shall bring the fatal hour.
Glide softly to thy rest then; Death should come
Gently, to one of gentle mould like thee,
As light winds wandering through groves of bloom
Detach the delicate blossom from the tree.
Close thy sweet eyes, calmly, and without pain;
And we will trust in God to see thee yet again.

———————•••———————

AN INDIAN STORY.

' I know where the timid fawn abides
In the depths of the shaded dell,
Where the leaves are broad and the thicket hides,
With its many stems and its tangled sides,
From the eye of the hunter well.

"I know where the young May violet grows,
    In its lone and lowly nook,
On the mossy bank, where the larch-tree throws
Its broad dark boughs, in solemn repose,
    Far over the silent brook.

"And that timid fawn starts not with fear
    When I steal to her secret bower;
And that young May violet to me is dear,
And I visit the silent streamlet near,
    To look on the lovely flower."

Thus Maquon sings as he lightly walks
    To the hunting-ground on the hills;
'Tis a song of his maid of the woods and rocks,
With her bright black eyes and long black locks,
    And voice like the music of rills.

He goes to the chase—but evil eyes
    Are at watch in the thicker shades;
For she was lovely that smiled on his sighs,
And he bore, from a hundred lovers, his prize,
    The flower of the forest maids.

The boughs in the morning wind are stirred,
    And the woods their song renew,
With the early carol of many a bird,
And the quickened tune of the streamlet heard
    Where the hazels trickle with dew.

And Maquon has promised his dark-haired maid,
    Ere eve shall redden the sky,
A good red deer from the forest shade,
That bounds with the herd through grove and glade,
    At her cabin-door shall lie.

The hollow woods, in the setting sun,
  Ring shrill with the fire-bird's lay;
And Maquon's sylvan labors are done,
And his shafts are spent, but the spoil they won
  He bears on his homeward way.

He stops near his bower—his eye perceives
  Strange traces along the ground—
At once to the earth his burden he heaves,
He breaks through the veil of boughs and leaves,
  And gains its door with a bound.

But the vines are torn on its walls that leant,
  And all from the young shrubs there
By struggling hands have the leaves been rent,
And there hangs on the sassafras, broken and bent,
  One tress of the well-known hair.

But where is she who, at this calm hour,
  Ever watched his coming to see?
She is not at the door, nor yet in the bower;
He calls—but he only hears on the flower
  The hum of the laden bee.

It is not a time for idle grief,
  Nor a time for tears to flow;
The horror that freezes his limbs is brief—
He grasps his war-axe and bow, and a sheaf
  Of darts made sharp for the foe.

And he looks for the print of the ruffian's feet,
  Where he bore the maiden away;
And he darts on the fatal path more fleet
Than the blast hurries the vapor and sleet
  O'er the wild November day.

'Twas early summer when Maquon's bride
　　Was stolen away from his door;
But at length the maples in crimson are dyed,
And the grape is black on the cabin side,—
　　And she smiles at his hearth once more.

But far in the pine-grove, dark and cold,
　　Where the yellow leaf falls not,
Nor the autumn shines in scarlet and gold,
There lies a hillock of fresh dark mould,
　　In the deepest gloom of the spot.

And the Indian girls, that pass that way,
　　Point out the ravisher's grave;
" And how soon to the bower she loved," they say,
" Returned the maid that was borne away
　　From Maquon, the fond and the brave."

SUMMER WIND.

It is a sultry day; the sun has drunk
The dew that lay upon the morning grass;
There is no rustling in the lofty elm
That canopies my dwelling, and its shade
Scarce cools me. All is silent, save the faint
And interrupted murmur of the bee,
Settling on the sick flowers, and then again
Instantly on the wing. The plants around
Feel the too potent fervors: the tall maize
Rolls up its long green leaves; the clover droops
Its tender foliage, and declines its blooms.
But far in the fierce sunshine tower the hills,

With all their growth of woods, silent and stern,
As if the scorching heat and dazzling light
Were but an element they loved. Bright clouds,
Motionless pillars of the brazen heaven,—
Their bases on the mountains—their white tops
Shining in the far ether—fire the air
With a reflected radiance, and make turn
The gazer's eye away. For me, I lie
Languidly in the shade, where the thick turf,
Yet virgin from the kisses of the sun,
Retains some freshness, and I woo the wind
That still delays his coming. Why so slow,
Gentle and voluble spirit of the air?
Oh, come and breathe upon the fainting earth
Coolness and life. Is it that in his caves
He hears me? See, on yonder woody ridge,
The pine is bending his proud top, and now
Among the nearer groves, chestnut and oak
Are tossing their green boughs about. He comes!
Lo, where the grassy meadow runs in waves!
The deep distressful silence of the scene
Breaks up with mingling of unnumbered sounds
And universal motion. He is come,
Shaking a shower of blossoms from the shrubs,
And bearing on their fragrance; and he brings
Music of birds, and rustling of young boughs,
And sound of swaying branches, and the voice
Of distant waterfalls. All the green herbs
Are stirring in his breath; a thousand flowers,
By the road-side and the borders of the brook,
Nod gayly to each other; glossy leaves
Are twinkling in the sun, as if the dew
Were on them yet, and silver waters break
Into small waves and sparkle as he comes.

AN INDIAN AT THE BURIAL-PLACE OF HIS FATHERS.

It is the spot I came to seek,—
  My fathers' ancient burial-place
Ere from these vales, ashamed and weak,
  Withdrew our wasted race.
It is the spot—I know it well—
Of which our old traditions tell.

For here the upland bank sends out
  A ridge toward the river-side;
I know the shaggy hills about,
  The meadows smooth and wide,
The plains, that, toward the southern sky,
Fenced east and west by mountains lie.

A white man, gazing on the scene,
  Would say a lovely spot was here,
And praise the lawns, so fresh and green,
  Between the hills so sheer.
I like it not—I would the plain
Lay in its tall old groves again.

The sheep are on the slopes around,
  The cattle in the meadows feed,
And laborers turn the crumbling ground,
  Or drop the yellow seed,
And prancing steeds, in trappings gay,
Whirl the bright chariot o'er the way.

Methinks it were a nobler sight
  To see these vales in woods arrayed,
Their summits in the golden light,
  Their trunks in grateful shade,
And herds of deer, that bounding go
O'er hills and prostrate trees below.

And then to mark the lord of all,
  The forest hero, trained to wars,
Quivered and plumed, and lithe and tall,
  And seamed with glorious scars,
Walk forth, amid his reign, to dare
The wolf, and grapple with the bear.

This bank, in which the dead were laid,
  Was sacred when its soil was ours;
Hither the silent Indian maid
  Brought wreaths of beads and flowers,
And the gray chief and gifted seer
Worshipped the god of thunders here.

But now the wheat is green and high
  On clods that hid the warrior's breast,
And scattered in the furrows lie
  The weapons of his rest;
And there, in the loose sand, is thrown
Of his large arm the mouldering bone.

Ah, little thought the strong and brave
  Who bore their lifeless chieftain forth—
Or the young wife that weeping gave
  Her first-born to the earth,
That the pale race, who waste us now,
Among their bones should guide the plough.

They waste us—ay—like April snow
  In the warm noon, we shrink away;
And fast they follow, as we go
  Towards the setting day,—

Till they shall fill the land, and we
Are driven into the western sea.

But I behold a fearful sign,
  To which the white men's eyes are blind;
Their race may vanish hence, like mine,
  And leave no trace behind,
Save ruins o'er the region spread,
And the white stones above the dead.

Before these fields were shorn and tilled,
  Full to the brim our rivers flowed;
The melody of waters filled
  The fresh and boundless wood;
And torrents dashed and rivulets played,
And fountains spouted in the shade.

Those grateful sounds are heard no more,
  The springs are silent in the sun;
The rivers, by the blackened shore,
  With lessening current run;
The realm our tribes are crushed to get
May be a barren desert yet.

SONG.

Dost thou idly ask to hear
  At what gentle seasons
Nymphs relent, when lovers near
  Press the tenderest reasons?
Ah, they give their faith too oft
  To the careless wooer;
Maidens' hearts are always soft:
  Would that men's were truer!

Woo the fair one, when around
  Early birds are singing;
When, o'er all the fragrant ground,
  Early herbs are springing:
When the brookside, bank, and grove,
  All with blossoms laden,
Shine with beauty, breathe of love,—
  Woo the timid maiden.

Woo her when, with rosy blush.
  Summer eve is sinking;
When, on rills that softly gush,
  Stars are softly winking;
When, through boughs that knit the bower,
  Moonlight gleams are stealing;
Woo her, till the gentle hour
  Wake a gentler feeling.

Woo her, when autumnal dyes
  Tinge the woody mountain;
When the dropping foliage lies
  In the weedy fountain;
Let the scene, that tells how fast
  Youth is passing over,
Warn her, ere her bloom is past,
  To secure her lover.

Woo her, when the north winds call
  At the lattice nightly;
When, within the cheerful hall,
  Blaze the fagots brightly;
While the wintry tempest round
  Sweeps the landscape hoary,
Sweeter in her ear shall sound
  Love's delightful story.

HYMN OF THE WALDENSES.

Hear, Father, hear thy faint afflicted flock
Cry to thee, from the desert and the rock;
While those, who seek to slay thy children, hold
Blasphemous worship under roofs of gold;
And the broad goodly lands, with pleasant airs
That nurse the grape and wave the grain, are theirs.

Yet better were this mountain wilderness,
And this wild life of danger and distress—
Watchings by night and perilous flight by day,
And meetings in the depths of earth to pray,
Better, far better, than to kneel with them,
And pay the impious rite thy laws condemn.

Thou, Lord, dost hold the thunder; the firm land
Tosses in billows when it feels thy hand;
Thou dashest nation against nation, then
Stillest the angry world to peace again.
Oh, touch their stony hearts who hunt thy sons—
The murderers of our wives and little ones.

Yet, mighty God, yet shall thy frown look forth
Unveiled, and terribly shall shake the earth.
Then the foul power of priestly sin and all
Its long-upheld idolatries shall fall.
Thou shalt raise up the trampled and oppressed,
And thy delivered saints shall dwell in rest.

MONUMENT MOUNTAIN.

Thou who wouldst see the lovely and the wild
Mingled in harmony on Nature's face,
Ascend our rocky mountains. Let thy foot
Fail not with weariness, for on their tops
The beauty and the majesty of earth,
Spread wide beneath, shall make thee to forget
The steep and toilsome way. There, as thou stand'st,
The haunts of men below thee, and around
The mountain summits, thy expanding heart
Shall feel a kindred with that loftier world
To which thou art translated, and partake
The enlargement of thy vision. Thou shalt look
Upon the green and rolling forest tops,
And down into the secrets of the glens,
And streams, that with their bordering thickets strive
To hide their windings. Thou shalt gaze, at once,
Here on white villages, and tilth, and herds,
And swarming roads, and there on solitudes
That only hear the torrent, and the wind,
And eagle's shriek. There is a precipice
That seems a fragment of some mighty wall,
Built by the hand that fashioned the old world,
To separate its nations, and thrown down
When the flood drowned them. To the north, a path
Conducts you up the narrow battlement.
Steep is the western side, shaggy and wild
With mossy trees, and pinnacles of flint,
And many a hanging crag. But, to the east,
Sheer to the vale go down the bare old cliffs,—
Huge pillars, that in middle heaven upbear
Their weather-beaten capitals, here dark

With moss the growth of centuries, and there
Of chalky whiteness where the thunderbolt
Has splintered them.   It is a fearful thing
To stand upon the beetling verge, and see
Where storm and lightning, from that huge gray wall,
Have tumbled down vast blocks, and at the base
Dashed them in fragments, and to lay thine ear
Over the dizzy depth, and hear the sound
Of winds, that struggle with the woods below,
Come up like ocean murmurs.   But the scene
Is lovely round; a beautiful river there
Wanders amid the fresh and fertile meads,
The paradise he made unto himself,
Mining the soil for ages.   On each side
The fields swell upward to the hills; beyond,
Above the hills, in the blue distance, rise
The mountain columns with which earth props heaven.

There is a tale about these reverend rocks,
A sad tradition of unhappy love,
And sorrows borne and ended, long ago,
When over these fair vales the savage sought
His game in the thick woods.   There was a maid,
The fairest of the Indian maids, bright-eyed,
With wealth of raven tresses, a light form,
And a gay heart.   About her cabin-door
The wide old woods resounded with her song
And fairy laughter all the summer day.
She loved her cousin; such a love was deemed,
By the morality of those stern tribes,
Incestuous, and she struggled hard and long
Against her love, and reasoned with her heart,
As simple Indian maiden might.   In vain.
Then her eye lost its lustre, and her step
Its lightness, and the gray-haired men that passed
Her dwelling, wondered that they heard no more
The accustomed song and laugh of her, whose looks
Were like the cheerful smile of Spring, they said,

Upon the Winter of their age. She went
To weep where no eye saw, and was not found
When all the merry girls were met to dance,
And all the hunters of the tribe were out;
Nor when they gathered from the rustling husk
The shining ear; nor when, by the river's side,
They pulled the grape and startled the wild shades
With sounds of mirth. The keen-eyed Indian dames
Would whisper to each other, as they saw
Her wasting form, and say *the girl will die.*

One day into the bosom of a friend,
A playmate of her young and innocent years,
She poured her griefs. "Thou know'st, and thou alone,"
She said, "for I have told thee all my love,
And guilt, and sorrow. I am sick of life.
All night I weep in darkness, and the morn
Glares on me, as upon a thing accursed,
That has no business on the earth. I hate
The pastimes and the pleasant toils that once
I loved; the cheerful voices of my friends
Sound in my ear like mockings, and, at night,
In dreams, my mother, from the land of souls,
Calls me and chides me. All that look on me
Do seem to know my shame; I cannot bear
Their eyes; I cannot from my heart root out
The love that wrings it so, and I must die."

It was a summer morning, and they went
To this old precipice. About the cliffs
Lay garlands, ears of maize, and shaggy skins
Of wolf and bear, the offerings of the tribe
Here made to the Great Spirit, for they deemed,
Like worshippers of the elder time, that God
Doth walk on the high places and affect
The earth-o'erlooking mountains. She had on
The ornaments with which her father loved
To deck the beauty of his bright-eyed girl,

And bade her wear when stranger warriors came
To be his guests.   Here the friends sat them down,
And sang, all day, old songs of love and death,
And decked the poor wan victim's hair with flowers,
And prayed that safe and swift might be her way
To the calm world of sunshine, where no grief
Makes the heart heavy and the eyelids red.
Beautiful lay the region of her tribe
Below her—waters resting in the embrace
Of the wide forest, and maize-planted glades
Opening amid the leafy wilderness.
She gazed upon it long, and at the sight
Of her own village peeping through the trees,
And her own dwelling, and the cabin roof
Of him she loved with an unlawful love,
And came to die for, a warm gush of tears
Ran from her eyes.   But when the sun grew low
And the hill shadows long, she threw herself
From the steep rock and perished.   There was scooped
Upon the mountain's southern slope, a grave;
And there they laid her, in the very garb
With which the maiden decked herself for death,
With the same withering wild flowers in her hair.
And o'er the mould that covered her, the tribe
Built up a simple monument, a cone
Of small loose stones.   Thenceforward all who passed,
Hunter, and dame, and virgin, laid a stone
In silence on the pile.   It stands there yet.
And Indians from the distant West, who come
To visit where their fathers' bones are laid,
Yet tell the sorrowful tale, and to this day
The mountain where the hapless maiden died
Is called the Mountain of the Monument.

AFTER A TEMPEST.

The day had been a day of wind and storm;
The wind was laid, the storm was overpast,
And stooping from the zenith bright and warm
Shone the great sun on the wide earth at last.
I stood upon the upland slope, and cast
Mine eye upon a broad and beauteous scene,
Where the vast plain lay girt by mountains vast,
And hills o'er hills lifted their heads of green,
With pleasant vales scooped out and villages between.

The rain-drops glistened on the trees around,
Whose shadows on the tall grass were not stirred,
Save when a shower of diamonds, to the ground,
Was shaken by the flight of startled bird;
For birds were warbling round, and bees were heard
About the flowers; the cheerful rivulet sung
And gossiped, as he hastened ocean-ward;
To the gray oak the squirrel, chiding, clung,
And chirping from the ground the grasshopper up-
    sprung.

And from beneath the leaves that kept them dry
Flew many a glittering insect here and there,
And darted up and down the butterfly,
That seemed a living blossom of the air
The flocks came scattering from the thicket, where
The violent rain had pent them; in the way
Strolled groups of damsels frolicksome and fair;
The farmer swung the scythe or turned the hay,
And 'twixt the heavy swaths his children were at
    play.

7

It was a scene of peace—and, like a spell,
Did that serene and golden sunlight fall
Upon the motionless wood that clothed the fell,
And precipice upspringing like a wall,
And glassy river and white waterfall,
And happy living things that trod the bright
And beauteous scene; while far beyond them all,
On many a lovely valley, out of sight,
Was poured from the blue heavens the same soft gold-
      en light.

I looked, and thought the quiet of the scene
An emblem of the peace that yet shall be,
When o'er earth's continents, and isles between,
The noise of war shall cease from sea to sea,
And married nations dwell in harmony;
When millions, crouching in the dust to one,
No more shall beg their lives on bended knee,
Nor the black stake be dressed, nor in the sun
The o'erlabored captive toil, and wish his life were
      done.

Too long, at clash of arms amid her bowers
And pools of blood, the earth has stood aghast,
The fair earth, that should only blush with flowers
And ruddy fruits; but not for aye can last
The storm, and sweet the sunshine when 'tis past.
Lo, the clouds roll away—they break—they fly,
And, like the glorious light of summer, cast
O'er the wide landscape from the embracing sky,
On all the peaceful world the smile of heaven shall
      lie.

AUTUMN WOODS.

Ere, in the northern gale,
The summer tresses of the trees are gone,
The woods of Autumn, all around our vale,
  Have put their glory on.

The mountains that infold,
In their wide sweep, the colored landscape round,
Seem groups of giant kings, in purple and gold,
  That guard the enchanted ground.

I roam the woods that crown
The upland, where the mingled splendors glow,
Where the gay company of trees look down
  On the green fields below.

My steps are not alone
In these bright walks; the sweet south-west, at play,
Flies, rustling, where the painted leaves are strown
  Along the winding way.

And far in heaven, the while,
The sun, that sends that gale to wander here,
Pours out on the fair earth his quiet smile,—
  The sweetest of the year.

Where now the solemn shade,
Verdure and gloom where many branches meet;
So grateful, when the noon of summer made
  The valleys sick with heat!

Let in through all the trees
Come the strange rays; the forest depths are bright;
Their sunny-colored foliage, in the breeze,
    Twinkles, like beams of light.

The rivulet, late unseen,
Where bickering through the shrubs its waters run,
Shines with the image of its golden screen
    And glimmerings of the sun.

But 'neath yon crimson tree,
Lover to listening maid might breathe his flame,
Nor mark, within its roseate canopy,
    Her blush of maiden shame.

Oh, Autumn! why so soon
Depart the hues that make thy forests glad,
Thy gentle wind and thy fair sunny noon,
    And leave thee wild and sad!

Ah! 'twere a lot too blest
For ever in thy colored shades to stray;
Amid the kisses of the soft south-west
    To rove and dream for aye;

And leave the vain low strife
That makes men mad—the tug for wealth and power,
The passions and the cares that wither life,
    And waste its little hour.

MUTATION.

They talk of short-lived pleasure—be it so—
   Pain dies as quickly: stern, hard-featured pain
Expires, and lets her weary prisoner go.
   The fiercest agonies have shortest reign ;
   And after dreams of horror, comes again
The welcome morning with its rays of peace.
   Oblivion, softly wiping out the stain,
Makes the strong secret pangs of shame to cease :·
Remorse is virtue's root ; its fair increase
   Are fruits of innocence and blessedness :
Thus joy, o'erborne and bound, doth still release
   His young limbs from the chains that round him press.
Weep not that the world changes—did it keep
A stable, changeless state, 'twere cause indeed to weep.

NOVEMBER.

Yet one smile more, departing, distant sun !
   One mellow smile through the soft vapory air,
Ere, o'er the frozen earth, the loud winds run,
   Or snows are sifted o'er the meadows bare.
One smile on the brown hills and naked trees,
   And the dark rocks whose summer wreaths are cast,
And the blue gentian flower, that, in the breeze,
   Nods lonely, of her beauteous race the last.

Yet a few sunny days, in which the bee
   Shall murmur by the hedge that skirts the way,
The cricket chirp upon the russet lea,
   And man delight to linger in thy ray.
Yet one rich smile, and we will try to bear
The piercing winter frost, and winds, and darkened air

SONG OF THE GREEK AMAZON.

I BUCKLE to my slender side
   The pistol and the scimitar,
And in my maiden flower and pride
   Am come to share the tasks of war.
And yonder stands my fiery steed,
   That paws the ground and neighs to go,
My charger of the Arab breed,—
   I took him from the routed foe.

My mirror is the mountain spring,
   At which I dress my ruffled hair;
My dimmed and dusty arms I bring,
   And wash away the blood-stain there.
Why should I guard from wind and sun
   This cheek, whose virgin rose is fled!
It was for one—oh, only one—
   I kept its bloom, and he is dead.

But they who slew him—unaware
   Of coward murderers lurking nigh—
And left him to the fowls of air,
   Are yet alive—and they must die.

They slew him—and my virgin years
   Are vowed to Greece and vengeance now,
And many an Othman dame, in tears,
   Shall rue the Grecian maiden's vow.

I touched the lute in better days,
   I led in dance the joyous band;
Ah! they may move to mirthful lays
   Whose hands can touch a lover's hand.
The march of hosts that haste to meet
   Seems gayer than the dance to me;
The lute's sweet tones are not so sweet
   As the fierce shout of victory.

TO A CLOUD.

Beautiful cloud! with folds so soft and fair,
   Swimming in the pure quiet air!
Thy fleeces bathed in sunlight, while below
   Thy shadow o'er the vale moves slow;
Where, midst their labor, pause the reaper train,
   As cool it comes along the grain.
Beautiful cloud! I would I were with thee
   In thy calm way o'er land and sea:
To rest on thy unrolling skirts, and look
   On Earth as on an open book;
On streams that tie her realms with silver bands,
   And the long ways that seam her lands;
And hear her humming cities, and the sound
   Of the great ocean breaking round.
Ay—I would sail, upon thy air-borne car,
   To blooming regions distant far,

To where the sun of Andalusia shines
  On his own olive-groves and vines,
Or the soft lights of Italy's clear sky
  In smiles upon her ruins lie.
But I would woo the winds to let us rest
  O'er Greece long fettered and oppressed,
Whose sons at length have heard the call that comes
  From the old battle-fields and tombs,
And risen, and drawn the sword, and on the foe
  Have dealt the swift and desperate blow,
And the Othman power is cloven, and the stroke
  Has touched its chains, and they are broke.
Ay, we would linger, till the sunset there
  Should come, to purple all the air,
And thou reflect upon the sacred ground
  The ruddy radiance streaming round.

Bright meteor! for the summer noontide made!
  Thy peerless beauty yet shall fade.
The sun, that fills with light each glistening fold,
  Shall set, and leave thee dark and cold:
The blast shall rend thy skirts, or thou may'st frown
  In the dark heaven when storms come down;
And weep in rain, till man's inquiring eye
  Miss thee, for ever, from the sky.

THE MURDERED TRAVELLER.

When spring, to woods and wastes around,
  Brought bloom and joy again,
The murdered traveller's bones were found,
  Far down a narrow glen.

THE MURDERED TRAVELLER.

The fragrant birch, above him, hung
  Her tassels in the sky;
And many a vernal blossom sprung,
  And nodded careless by.

The red-bird warbled, as he wrought
  His hanging nest o'erhead,
And fearless, near the fatal spot,
  Her young the partridge led.

But there was weeping far away,
  And gentle eyes, for him,
With watching many an anxious day,
  Were sorrowful and dim.

They little knew, who loved him so,
  The fearful death he met,
When shouting o'er the desert snow,
  Unarmed, and hard beset;—

Nor how, when round the frosty pole
  The northern dawn was red,
The mountain wolf and wild-cat stole
  To banquet on the dead;—

Nor how, when strangers found his bones,
  They dressed the hasty bier,
And marked his grave with nameless stones,
  Unmoistened by a tear.

But long they looked, and feared, and wept,
  Within his distant home;
And dreamed, and started as they slept,
  For joy that he was come.

Long, long they looked—but never spied
  His welcome step again,
Nor knew the fearful death he died
  Far down that narrow glen.

HYMN TO THE NORTH STAR.

THE sad and solemn night
Hath yet her multitude of cheerful fires;
The glorious host of light
Walk the dark hemisphere till she retires;
All through her silent watches, gliding slow,
Her constellations come, and climb the heavens, and go.

Day, too, hath many a star
To grace his gorgeous reign, as bright as they:
Through the blue fields afar,
Unseen, they follow in his flaming way:
Many a bright lingerer, as the eve grows dim,
Tells what a radiant troop arose and set with him.

And thou dost see them rise,
Star of the Pole! and thou dost see them set.
Alone, in thy cold skies,
Thou keep'st thy old unmoving station yet,
Nor join'st the dances of that glittering train,
Nor dipp'st thy virgin orb in the blue western main.

There, at morn's rosy birth,
Thou lookest meekly through the kindling air,
And eve, that round the earth
Chases the day, beholds thee watching there;
There noontide finds thee, and the hour that calls
The shapes of polar flame to scale heaven's azure walls.

Alike, beneath thine eye,
The deeds of darkness and of light are done;
High towards the star-lit sky
Towns blaze, the smoke of battle blots the sun,

The night-storm on a thousand hills is loud,
And the strong wind of day doth mingle sea and cloud.

    On thy unaltering blaze
The half-wrecked mariner, his compass lost,
    Fixes his steady gaze,
And steers, undoubting, to the friendly coast;
And they who stray in perilous wastes, by night,
Are glad when thou dost shine to guide their foot-
    steps right.

    And, therefore, bards of old,
Sages and hermits of the solemn wood,
    Did in thy beams behold
A beauteous type of that unchanging good,
That bright eternal beacon, by whose ray
The voyager of time should shape his heedful way.

THE LAPSE OF TIME.

Lament who will, in fruitless tears,
    The speed with which our moments fly;
I sigh not over vanished years,
    But watch the years that hasten by.

Look, how they come,—a mingled crowd
    Of bright and dark, but rapid days;
Beneath them, like a summer cloud,
    The wide world changes as I gaze.

What! grieve that time has brought so soon
    The sober age of manhood on!
As idly might I weep, at noon,
    To see the blush of morning gone.

Could I give up the hopes that glow
  In prospect like Elysian isles;
And let the cheerful future go,
  With all her promises and smiles?

The future!—cruel were the power
  Whose doom would tear thee from my heart,
Thou sweetener of the present hour!
  We cannot—no—we will not part.

Oh, leave me, still, the rapid flight
  That makes the changing seasons gay,
The grateful speed that brings the night,
  The swift and glad return of day;

The months that touch, with added grace,
  This little prattler at my knee,
In whose arch eye and speaking face
  New meaning every hour I see;

The years, that o'er each sister land
  Shall lift the country of my birth,
And nurse her strength, till she shall stand
  The pride and pattern of the earth:

Till younger commonwealths, for aid,
  Shall cling about her ample robe,
And from her frown shall shrink afraid
  The crowned oppressors of the globe.

True—time will seam and blanch my brow—
  Well—I shall sit with aged men,
And my good glass will tell me how
  A grizzly beard becomes me then.

And then, should no dishonor lie
  Upon my head, when I am gray,
Love yet shall watch my fading eye,
  And smooth the path of my decay.

Then haste thee, Time—'tis kindness all
  That speeds thy winged feet so fast:
Thy pleasures stay not till they pall,
  And all thy pains are quickly past.

Thou fliest and bear'st away our woes,
  And as thy shadowy train depart,
The memory of sorrow grows
  A lighter burden on the heart.

SONG OF THE STARS.

When the radiant morn of creation broke,
And the world in the smile of God awoke,
And the empty realms of darkness and death
Were moved through their depths by his mighty
      breath,
And orbs of beauty and spheres of flame
From the void abyss by myriads came,—
In the joy of youth as they darted away,
Through the widening wastes of space to play,
Their silver voices in chorus rang,
And this was the song the bright ones sang:

" Away, away, through the wide, wide sky,
  The fair blue fields that before us lie,—
Each sun with the worlds that round him roll,
Each planet, poised on her turning pole;

8

With her isles of green, and her clouds of white,
And her waters that lie like fluid light.

"For the source of glory uncovers his face,
And the brightness o'erflows unbounded space;
And we drink as we go the luminous tides
In our ruddy air and our blooming sides:
Lo, yonder the living splendors play;
Away, on our joyous path, away!

"Look, look, through our glittering ranks afar,
In the infinite azure, star after star,
How they brighten and bloom as they swiftly pass!
How the verdure runs o'er each rolling mass!
And the path of the gentle winds is seen,
Where the small waves dance, and the young woods
        lean.

"And see where the brighter day-beams pour,
How the rainbows hang in the sunny shower;
And the morn and eve, with their pomp of hues,
Shift o'er the bright planets and shed their dews;
And 'twixt them both, o'er the teeming ground,
With her shadowy cone the night goes round!

"Away, away! in our blossoming bowers,
In the soft air wrapping these spheres of ours,
In the seas and fountains that shine with morn,
See, Love is brooding, and Life is born,
And breathing myriads are breaking from night,
To rejoice, like us, in motion and light.

"Glide on in your beauty, ye youthful spheres,
To weave the dance that measures the years;
Glide on, in the glory and gladness sent,
To the furthest wall of the firmament,—
The boundless visible smile of Him,
To the veil of whose brow your lamps are dim."

A FOREST HYMN.

THE groves were God's first temples. Ere man learned
To hew the shaft, and lay the architrave,
And spread the roof above them,—ere he framed
The lofty vault, to gather and roll back
The sound of anthems; in the darkling wood,
Amidst the cool and silence, he knelt down,
And offered to the Mightiest solemn thanks
And supplication.   For his simple heart
Might not resist the sacred influences
Which, from the stilly twilight of the place,
And from the gray old trunks that high in heaven
Mingled their mossy boughs, and from the sound
Of the invisible breath that swayed at once
All their green tops, stole over him, and bowed
His spirit with the thought of boundless power
And inaccessible majesty.   Ah, why
Should we, in the world's riper years, neglect
God's ancient sanctuaries, and adore
Only among the crowd, and under roofs
That our frail hands have raised?   Let me, at least,
Here, in the shadow of this aged wood,
Offer one hymn—thrice happy, if it find
Acceptance in His ear.

               Father, thy hand
Hath reared these venerable columns, thou
Didst weave this verdant roof.   Thou didst look down
Upon the naked earth, and, forthwith, rose
All these fair ranks of trees.   They, in thy sun,
Budded, and shook their green leaves in thy breeze,
And shot towards heaven.   The century-living crow,
Whose birth was in their tops, grew old and died

Among their branches, till, at last, they stood,
As now they stand, massy, and tall, and dark,
Fit shrine for humble worshipper to hold
Communion with his Maker.   These dim vaults,
These winding aisles, of human pomp or pride
Report not.   No fantastic carvings show
The boast of our vain race to change the form
Of thy fair works.   But thou art here—thou fill'st
The solitude.   Thou art in the soft winds
That run along the summit of these trees
In music; thou art in the cooler breath
That from the inmost darkness of the place
Comes, scarcely felt; the barky trunks, the ground,
The fresh moist ground, are all instinct with thee.
Here is continual worship;—nature, here,
In the tranquillity that thou dost love,
Enjoys thy presence.   Noiselessly, around,
From perch to perch, the solitary bird
Passes; and yon clear spring, that, midst its herbs,
Wells softly forth and wandering steeps the roots
Of half the mighty forest, tells no tale
Of all the good it does.   Thou hast not left
Thyself without a witness, in these shades,
Of thy perfections.   Grandeur, strength, and grace
Are here to speak of thee.   This mighty oak—
By whose immovable stem I stand and seem
Almost annihilated—not a prince,
In all that proud old world beyond the deep,
E'er wore his crown as loftily as he
Wears the green coronal of leaves with which
Thy hand has graced him.   Nestled at his root
Is beauty, such as blooms not in the glare
Of the broad sun.   That delicate forest flower
With scented breath, and look so like a smile,
Seems, as it issues from the shapeless mould,
An emanation of the indwelling Life,
A visible token of the upholding Love,
That are the soul of this wide universe.

My heart is awed within me when I think
Of the great miracle that still goes on,
In silence, round me—the perpetual work
Of thy creation, finished, yet renewed
For ever.   Written on thy works I read
The lesson of thy own eternity.
Lo! all grow old and die—but see again,
How on the faltering footsteps of decay
Youth presses—ever gay and beautiful youth
In all its beautiful forms.   These lofty trees
Wave not less proudly that their ancestors
Moulder beneath them.   Oh, there is not lost
One of earth's charms: upon her bosom yet,
After the flight of untold centuries,
The freshness of her far beginning lies
And yet shall lie.   Life mocks the idle hate
Of his arch enemy Death—yea, seats himself
Upon the tyrant's throne—the sepulchre,
And of the triumphs of his ghastly foe
Makes his own nourishment.   For he came forth
From thine own bosom, and shall have no end.

There have been holy men who hid themselves
Deep in the woody wilderness, and gave
Their lives to thought and prayer, till they outlived
The generation born with them, nor seemed
Less aged than the hoary trees and rocks
Around them;—and there have been holy men
Who deemed it were not well to pass life thus.
But let me often to these solitudes
Retire, and in thy presence reassure
My feeble virtue.   Here its enemies,
The passions, at thy plainer footsteps shrink
And tremble and are still.   Oh, God! when thou
Dost scare the world with tempests, set on fire
The heavens with falling thunderbolts, or fill,
With all the waters of the firmament,
The swift dark whirlwind that uproots the woods

And drowns the villages; when, at thy call,
Uprises the great deep and throws himself
Upon the continent, and overwhelms
Its cities—who forgets not, at the sight   .
Of these tremendous tokens of thy power,
His pride, and lays his strifes and follies by!
Oh, from these sterner aspects of thy face
Spare me and mine, nor let us need the wrath
Of the mad unchained elements to teach
Who rules them.   Be it ours to meditate,
In these calm shades, thy milder majesty,
And to the beautiful order of thy works
Learn to conform the order of our lives.

———◆◆———

"OH FAIREST OF THE RURAL MAIDS."

Oh fairest of the rural maids!
Thy birth was in the forest shades;
Green boughs, and glimpses of the sky,
Were all that met thine infant eye.

Thy sports, thy wanderings, when a child,
Were ever in the sylvan wild;
And all the beauty of the place
Is in thy heart and on thy face.

The twilight of the trees and rocks
Is in the light shade of thy locks;
Thy step is as the wind, that weaves
Its playful way among the leaves.

Thine eyes are springs, in whose serene
And silent waters heaven is seen;
Their lashes are the herbs that look
On their young figures in the brook.

The forest depths, by foot unpressed,
Are not more sinless than thy breast;
The holy peace, that fills the air
Of those calm solitudes. is there.

———•••———

"I BROKE THE SPELL THAT HELD ME LONG."

I BROKE the spell that held me long,
The dear, dear witchery of song.
I said, the poet's idle lore
Shall waste my prime of years no more,
For Poetry, though heavenly born,
Consorts with poverty and scorn

I broke the spell—nor deemed its power
Could fetter me another hour.
Ah, thoughtless! how could I forget
Its causes were around me yet?
For wheresoe'er I looked, the while,
Was nature's everlasting smile.

Still came and lingered on my sight
Of flowers and streams the bloom and light,
And glory of the stars and sun;—
And these and poetry are one.
They, ere the world had held me long,
Recalled me to the love of song.

JUNE.

I GAZED upon the glorious sky
    And the green mountains round;
And thought that when I came to lie
    At rest within the ground,
'Twere pleasant, that in flowery June,
When brooks send up a cheerful tune,
    And groves a joyous sound,
The sexton's hand, my grave to make,
The rich, green mountain turf should break.

A cell within the frozen mould,
    A coffin borne through sleet,
And icy clods above it rolled,
    While fierce the tempests beat—
Away!—I will not think of these—
Blue be the sky and soft the breeze,
    Earth green beneath the feet,
And be the damp mould gently pressed
Into my narrow place of rest.

There through the long, long summer hours,
    The golden light should lie,
And thick young herbs and groups of flowers
    Stand in their beauty by.
The oriole should build and tell
His love-tale close beside my cell;
    The idle butterfly
Should rest him there, and there be heard
The housewife bee and humming-bird.

And what if cheerful shouts at noon
 Come, from the village sent,
Or songs of maids, beneath the moon
 With fairy laughter blent!
And what if, in the evening light,
Betrothed lovers walk in sight
 Of my low monument!
I would the lovely scene around
Might know no sadder sight nor sound.

I know, I know I should not see
 The season's glorious show,
Nor would its brightness shine for me,
 Nor its wild music flow;
But if, around my place of sleep,
The friends I love should come to weep,
 They might not haste to go.
Soft airs, and song, and light, and bloom,
Should keep them lingering by my tomb.

These to their softened hearts should bear
 The thought of what has been,
And speak of one who cannot share
 The gladness of the scene;
Whose part, in all the pomp that fills
The circuit of the summer hills,
 Is—that his grave is green;
And deeply would their hearts rejoice
To hear again his living voice.

A SONG OF PITCAIRN'S ISLAND.

Come, take our boy, and we will go
    Before our cabin door;
The winds shall bring us, as they blow,
    The murmurs of the shore;
And we will kiss his young blue eyes,
And I will sing him, as he lies,
    Songs that were made of yore:
I'll sing, in his delighted ear,
The island lays thou lov'st to hear.

And thou, while stammering I repeat,
    Thy country's tongue shalt teach;
'Tis not so soft, but far more sweet
    Than my own native speech:
For thou no other tongue didst know,
When, scarcely twenty moons ago,
    Upon Tahete's beach,
Thou cam'st to woo me to be thine,
With many a speaking look and sign.

I knew thy meaning—thou didst praise
    My eyes, my locks of jet;
Ah! well for me they won thy gaze,—
    But thine were fairer yet!
I'm glad to see my infant wear
Thy soft blue eyes and sunny hair,
    And when my sight is met
By his white brow and blooming cheek,
I feel a joy I cannot speak.

Come talk of Europe's maids with me,
    Whose necks and cheeks, they tell,
Outshine the beauty of the sea,
    White foam and crimson shell.
I'll shape like theirs my simple dress,
And bind like them each jetty tress,
    A sight to please thee well:
And for my dusky brow will braid
A bonnet like an English maid.

Come, for the soft low sunlight calls,
    We lose the pleasant hours;
'Tis lovelier than these cottage walls,—
    That seat among the flowers.
And I will learn of thee a prayer,
To Him who gave a home so fair,
    A lot so blest as ours—
The God who made, for thee and me,
This sweet lone isle amid the sea.

———•••———

THE FIRMAMENT.

Ay! gloriously thou standest there,
    Beautiful, boundless firmament!
That, swelling wide o'er earth and air,
    And round the horizon bent,
With thy bright vault, and sapphire wall,
Dost overhang and circle all.

Far, far below thee, tall gray trees
    Arise, and piles built up of old,
And hills, whose ancient summits freeze
    In the fierce light and cold.

The eagle soars his utmost height,
Yet far thou stretchest o'er his flight.

Thou hast thy frowns—with thee on high
  The storm has made his airy seat,
Beyond that soft blue curtain lie
  His stores of hail and sleet.
Thence the consuming lightnings break,
There the strong hurricanes awake.

Yet art thou prodigal of smiles—
  Smiles, sweeter than thy frowns are stern·
Earth sends, from all her thousand isles,
  A shout at their return.
The glory that comes down from thee,
Bathes, in deep joy, the land and sea.

The sun, the gorgeous sun is thine,
  The pomp that brings and shuts the day,
The clouds that round him change and shine,
  The airs that fan his way.
Thence look the thoughtful stars, and there
The meek moon walks the silent air.

The sunny Italy may boast
  The beauteous tints that flush her skies,
And lovely, round the Grecian coast,
  May thy blue pillars rise.
I only know how fair they stand
Around my own beloved laud.

And they are fair—a charm is theirs,
  That earth, the proud green earth, has not—
With all the forms, and hues, and airs,
  That haunt her sweetest spot.
We gaze upon thy calm pure sphere,
And read of Heaven's eternal year.

Oh, when, amid the throng of men,
  The heart grows sick of hollow mirth,
How willingly we turn us then
  Away from this cold earth,
And look into thy azure breast,
For seats of innocence and rest!

———•••———

"I CANNOT FORGET WITH WHAT FERVID DEVOTION."

I CANNOT forget with what fervid devotion
  I worshipped the visions of verse and of fame:
Each gaze at the glories of earth, sky, and ocean,
  To my kindled emotions, was wind over flame.

And deep were my musings in life's early blossom,
  Mid the twilight of mountain groves wandering
    long;
How thrilled my young veins, and how throbbed my
    full bosom,
  When o'er me descended the spirit of song.

'Mong the deep-cloven fells that for ages had listened
  To the rush of the pebble-paved river between,
Where the kingfisher screamed and gray precipice
    glistened,
  All breathless with awe have I gazed on the scene;

Till I felt the dark power o'er my reveries stealing,
  From the gloom of the thickets that over me hung,
And the thoughts that awoke, in that rapture of feeling,
  Were formed into verse as they rose to my tongue.

9

Bright visions! I mixed with the world, and ye faded
   No longer your pure rural worshipper now;
In the haunts your continual presence pervaded,
   Ye shrink from the signet of care on my brow.

In the old mossy groves on the breast of the mountain
   In deep lonely glens where the waters complain,
By the shade of the rock, by the gush of the fountain,
   I seek your loved footsteps, but seek them in vain.

Oh, leave not, forlorn and for ever forsaken,
   Your pupil and victim to life and its tears!
But sometimes return, and in mercy awaken
   The glories ye showed to his earlier years.

TO A MUSQUITO.

Fair insect! that, with threadlike legs spread out,
   And blood-extracting bill and filmy wing, .
Does murmur, as thou slowly sail'st about,
   In pitiless ears full many a plaintive thing,
And tell how little our large veins would bleed,
Would we but yield them to thy bitter need.

Unwillingly, I own, and, what is worse,
   Full angrily men hearken to thy plaint;
Thou gettest many a brush, and many a curse,
   For saying thou art gaunt, and starved, and faint:
Even the old beggar, while he asks for food,
Would kill thee, hapless stranger, if he could.

I call thee stranger, for the town, I ween,
  Has not the honor of so proud a birth,—
Thou com'st from Jersey meadows, fresh and green,
  The offspring of the gods, though born on earth;
For Titan was thy sire, and fair was she,
The ocean nymph that nursed thy infancy.

Beneath the rushes was thy cradle swung,
  And when at length thy gauzy wings grew strong,
Abroad to gentle airs their folds were flung,
  Rose in the sky and bore thee soft along;
The south wind breathed to waft thee on thy way,
And danced and shone beneath the billowy bay.

Calm rose afar the city spires, and thence
  Came the deep murmur of its throng of men,
And as its grateful odors met thy sense,
  They seemed the perfumes of thy native fen.
Fair lay its crowded streets, and at the sight
Thy tiny song grew shriller with delight.

At length thy pinions fluttered in Broadway—
  Ah, there were fairy steps, and white necks kissed
By wanton airs, and eyes whose killing ray
  Shone through the snowy veils like stars through
    mist;
And fresh as morn, on many a cheek and chin,
Bloomed the bright blood through the transparent
  skin.

Sure these were sights to touch an anchorite!
  What! do I hear thy slender voice complain!
Thou wailest, when I talk of beauty's light,
  As if it brought the memory of pain:
Thou art a wayward being—well—come near,
And pour thy tale of sorrow in my ear.

What sayst thou—slanderer!—rouge makes thee sick!
  And China bloom at best is sorry food!
And Rowland's Kalydor, if laid on thick,
  Poisons the thirsty wretch that bores for blood!
Go! 'twas a just reward that met thy crime—
But shun the sacrilege another time.

That bloom was made to look at, not to touch;
  To worship, not approach, that radiant white;
And well might sudden vengeance light on such
  As dared, like thee, most impiously to bite.
Thou shouldst have gazed at distance and admired,
Murmured thy adoration and retired.

Thou'rt welcome to the town—but why come here
  To bleed a brother poet, gaunt like thee?
Alas! the little blood I have is dear,
  And thin will be the banquet drawn from me.
Look round—the pale-eyed sisters in my cell,
Thy old acquaintance, Song and Famine, dwell.

Try some plump alderman, and suck the blood
  Enriched by generous wine and costly meat;
On well-filled skins, sleek as thy native mud,
  Fix thy light pump and press thy freckled feet
Go to the men for whom, in ocean's halls,
The oyster breeds, and the green turtle sprawls

There corks are drawn, and the red vintage flows
  To fill the swelling veins for thee, and now
The ruddy cheek and now the ruddier nose
  Shall tempt thee, as thou flittest round the brow;
And when the hour of sleep its quiet brings,
No angry hand shall rise to brush thy wings.

LINES ON REVISITING THE COUNTRY.

I STAND upon my native hills again,
　Broad, round, and green, that in the summer sky
With garniture of waving grass and grain,
　Orchards, and beechen forests, basking lie,
While deep the sunless glens are scooped between,
Where brawl o'er shallow beds the streams unseen.

A lisping voice and glancing eyes are near,
　And ever restless feet of one, who, now,
Gathers the blossoms of her fourth bright year;
　There plays a gladness o'er her fair young brow,
As breaks the varied scene upon her sight,
Upheaved and spread in verdure and in light.

For I have taught her, with delighted eye,
　To gaze upon the mountains,—to behold,
With deep affection, the pure ample sky,
　And clouds along its blue abysses rolled,—
To love the song of waters, and to hear
The melody of winds with charmed ear.

Here, I have 'scaped the city's stifling heat,
　Its horrid sounds, and its polluted air;
And, where the season's milder fervors beat,
　And gales, that sweep the forest borders, bear
The song of bird, and sound of running stream,
Am come awhile to wander and to dream.

Ay, flame thy fiercest, sun! thou canst not wake,
　In this pure air, the plague that walks unseen.
The maize leaf and the maple bough but take,
　From thy strong heats, a deeper, glossier green.

The mountain wind, that faints not in thy ray,
Sweeps the blue steams of pestilence away.

The mountain wind! most spiritual thing of all
   The wide earth knows; when, in the sultry time,
He stoops him from his vast cerulean hall,
   He seems the breath of a celestial clime!
As if from heaven's wide-open gates did flow
Health and refreshment on the world below.

THE DEATH OF THE FLOWERS.

The melancholy days are come, the saddest of the year,
Of wailing winds, and naked woods, and meadows
    brown and sere.
Heaped in the hollows of the grove, the autumn leaves
    lie dead;
They rustle to the eddying gust, and to the rabbit's tread.
The robin and the wren are flown, and from the shrubs
    the jay,
And from the wood-top calls the crow through all the
    gloomy day.

Where are the flowers, the fair young flowers, that
    lately sprang and stood
In brighter light, and softer airs, a beauteous sisterhood!
Alas! they all are in their graves, the gentle race of
    flowers
Are lying in their lowly beds, with the fair and good
    of ours.
The rain is falling where they lie, but the cold No-
    vember rain
Calls not from out the gloomy earth the lovely ones
    again.

The wind-flower and the violet, they perished long
    ago,
And the brier-rose and the orchis died amid the sum-
    mer glow;
But on the hill the golden-rod, and the aster in the
    wood,
And the yellow sun-flower by the brook in autumn
    beauty stood,
Till fell the frost from the clear cold heaven, as falls
    the plague on men,
And the brightness of their smile was gone, from up-
    land, glade, and glen.

And now, when comes the calm mild day, as still such
    days will come,
To call the squirrel and the bee from out their winter
    home;
When the sound of dropping nuts is heard, though
    all the trees are still,
And twinkle in the smoky light the waters of the rill,
The south wind searches for the flowers whose fra-
    grance late he bore,
And sighs to find them in the wood and by the
    stream no more.

And then I think of one who in her youthful beauty
    died,
The fair meek blossom that grew up and faded by my
    side:
In the cold moist earth we laid her, when the forests
    cast the leaf,
And we wept that one so lovely should have a life so
    brief:
Yet not unmeet it was that one, like that young friend
    of ours,
So gentle and so beautiful, should perish with the
    flowers.

ROMERO.

When freedom, from the land of Spain,
  By Spain's degenerate sons was driven,
Who gave their willing limbs again
  To wear the chain so lately riven;
Romero broke the sword he wore—
" Go, faithful brand," the warrior said,
" Go, undishonored, never more
  The blood of man shall make thee red:
  I grieve for that already shed;
And I am sick at heart to know,
That faithful friend and noble foe
Have only bled to make more strong
The yoke that Spain has worn so long.
Wear it who will, in abject fear—
  I wear it not who have been free;
The perjured Ferdinand shall hear
  No oath of loyalty from me."
Then, hunted by the hounds of power,
  Romero chose a safe retreat,
Where bleak Nevada's summits tower
  Above the beauty at their feet.
There once, when on his cabin lay
The crimson light of setting day,
When even on the mountain's breast
The chainless winds were all at rest,
And he could hear the river's flow
From the calm paradise below;
Warmed with his former fires again,
He framed this rude but solemn strain:

I.

" Here will I make my home—for here at least I see,
Upon this wild Sierra's side, the steps of Liberty;
Where the locust chirps unscared beneath the un-
    pruned lime,
And the merry bee doth hide from man the spoil of
    the mountain thyme;
Where the pure winds come and go, and the wild
    vine strays at will,
An outcast from the haunts of men, she dwells with
    Nature still.

II.

" I see the valleys, Spain! where thy mighty rivers
    run,
And the hills that lift thy harvests and vineyards to
    the sun,
And the flocks that drink thy brooks and sprinkle all
    the green,
Where lie thy plains, with sheep-walks seamed, and
    olive-shades between:
I see thy fig-trees bask, with the fair pomegranate
    near,
And the fragrance of thy lemon-groves can almost
    reach me here.

III.

" Fair—fair—but fallen Spain! 'tis with a swelling
    heart,
That I think on all thou mightst have been, and look
    at what thou art;
But the strife is over now, and all the good and brave.
That would have raised thee up, are gone, to exile or
    the grave.
Thy fleeces are for monks, thy grapes for the convent
    feast,
And the wealth of all thy harvest-fields for the pam-
    pered lord and priest.

IV.

"But I shall see the day—it will come before I
    die—
I shall see it in my silver hairs, and with an age-
    dimmed eye;—
When the spirit of the land to liberty shall bound,
As yonder fountain leaps away from the darkness of
    the ground:
And to my mountain cell, the voices of the free
Shall rise, as from the beaten shore the thunders of
    the sea."

---◆◆◆---

A MEDITATION ON RHODE-ISLAND COAL.

Decolor, obscurus, vilis, non ille repexam
Cæsariem regum, non candida virginis ornat
Colla, nec insigni splendet per cingula morsu.
Sed nova si nigri videas miracula saxi,
Tunc superat pulchros cultus et quicquid Eois
Indus litoribus rubrâ scrutatur in algâ.
                                        CLAUDIAN.

I SAT beside the glowing grate, fresh heaped
    With Newport coal, and as the flame grew bright
—The many-colored flame—and played and leaped,
    I thought of rainbows and the northern light,
Moore's Lalla Rookh, the Treasury Report,
And other brilliant matters of the sort.

And last I thought of that fair isle which sent
    The mineral fuel; on a summer day
I saw it once, with heat and travel spent,
    And scratched by dwarf-oaks in the hollow way;
Now dragged through sand, now jolted over stone—
A rugged road through rugged Tiverton.

And hotter grew the air, and hollower grew
　The deep-worn path, and horror-struck, I thought,
Where will this dreary passage lead me to?
　This long dull road, so narrow, deep, and hot?
I looked to see it dive in earth outright;
I looked—but saw a far more welcome sight.

Like a soft mist upon the evening shore,
　At once a lovely isle before me lay,
Smooth and with tender verdure covered o'er,
　As if just risen from its calm inland bay;
Sloped each way gently to the grassy edge,
And the small waves that dallied with the sedge.

The barley was just reaped—its heavy sheaves
　Lay on the stubble field—the tall maize stood
Dark in its summer growth, and shook its leaves—
　And bright the sunlight played on the young wood—
For fifty years ago, the old men say,
The Briton hewed their ancient groves away.

I saw where fountains freshened the green land,
　And where the pleasant road, from door to door,
With rows of cherry-trees on either hand,
　Went wandering all that fertile region o'er—
Rogue's Island once—but when the rogues were dead,
Rhode Island was the name it took instead.

Beautiful island! then it only seemed
　A lovely stranger—it has grown a friend.
I gazed on its smooth slopes, but never dreamed
　How soon that green and quiet isle would send
The treasures of its womb across the sea,
To warm a poet's room and boil his tea.

Dark anthracite! that reddenest on my hearth,
　Thou in those island mines didst slumber long;
But now thou art come forth to move the earth,
　And put to shame the men that mean thee wrong.

Thou shalt be coals of fire to those that hate thee,
And warm the shins of all that underrate thee.

Yea, they did wrong thee foully—they who mocked
    Thy honest face, and said thou wouldst not burn;
Of hewing thee to chimney-pieces talked,
    And grew profane—and swore, in bitter scorn,
That men might to thy inner caves retire,
And there, unsinged, abide the day of fire.

Yet is thy greatness nigh.   I pause to state,
    That I too have seen greatness—even I—
Shook hands with Adams—stared at La Fayette,
    When, barehead, in the hot noon of July,
He would not let the umbrella be held o'er him,
For which three cheers burst from the mob before him.

And I have seen—not many months ago—
    An eastern Governor in chapeau bras
And military coat, a glorious show!
    Ride forth to visit the reviews, and ah!
How oft he smiled and bowed to Jonathan!
How many hands were shook and votes were won!

'Twas a great Governor—thou too shalt be
    Great in thy turn—and wide shall spread thy fame
And swiftly; furthest Maine shall hear of thee,
    And cold New Brunswick gladden at thy name,
And, faintly through its sleets, the weeping isle
That sends the Boston folks their cod shall smile.

For thou shalt forge vast railways, and shalt heat
    The hissing rivers into steam, and drive
Huge masses from thy mines, on iron feet,
    Walking their steady way, as if alive,
Northward, till everlasting ice besets thee,
And south as far as the grim Spaniard lets thee.

Thou shalt make mighty engines swim the sea,
  Like its own monsters—boats that for a guinea
Will take a man to Havre—and shalt be
  The moving soul of many a spinning-jenny,
And ply thy shuttles, till a bard can wear
As good a suit of broadcloth as the mayor.

Then we will laugh at winter when we hear
  The grim old churl about our dwellings rave:
Thou, from that "ruler of the inverted year,"
  Shalt pluck the knotty sceptre Cowper gave,
And pull him from his sledge, and drag him in,
And melt the icicles from off his chin.

-----•••-----

THE NEW MOON.

When, as the garish day is done,
Heaven burns with the descended sun,
    'Tis passing sweet to mark,
Amid that flush of crimson light,
The new moon's modest bow grow bright,
    As earth and sky grow dark.

Few are the hearts too cold to feel
A thrill of gladness o'er them steal,
    When first the wandering eye
Sees faintly, in the evening blaze,
That glimmering curve of tender rays
    Just planted in the sky.

The sight of that young crescent brings
Thoughts of all fair and youthful things—
    The hopes of early years;

10

And childhood's purity and grace,
And joys that like a rainbow chase
   The passing shower of tears.

The captive yields him to the dream
Of freedom, when that virgin beam
   Comes out upon the air:
And painfully the sick man tries
To fix his dim and burning eyes
   On the soft promise there.

Most welcome to the lover's sight,
Glitters that pure, emerging light;
   For prattling poets say,
That sweetest is the lovers' walk,
And tenderest is their murmured talk,
   Beneath its gentle ray.

And there do graver men behold
A type of errors, loved of old,
   Forsaken and forgiven;
And thoughts and wishes not of earth,
Just opening in their early birth,
   Like that new light in heaven.

OCTOBER.

Ay, thou art welcome, heaven's delicious breath,
  When woods begin to wear the crimson leaf,
  And suns grow meek, and the meek suns grow brief,
And the year smiles as it draws near its death.

Wind of the sunny south! oh, still delay
  In the gay woods and in the golden air,
  Like to a good old age released from care,
Journeying, in long serenity, away.
In such a bright, late quiet, would that I
  Might wear out life like thee, mid bowers and brooks,
  And, dearer yet, the sunshine of kind looks,
And music of kind voices ever nigh;
And when my last sand twinkled in the glass,
Pass silently from men, as thou dost pass.

———————•••———————

THE DAMSEL OF PERU.

WHERE olive leaves were twinkling in every wind
      that blew,
There sat beneath the pleasant shade a damsel of Peru.
Betwixt the slender boughs, as they opened to the air,
Came glimpses of her ivory neck and of her glossy hair;
And sweetly rang her silver voice, within that shady
      nook,
As from the shrubby glen is heard the sound of hid-
      den brook.

'Tis a song of love and valor, in the noble Spanish
      tongue,
That once upon the sunny plains of old Castile was
      sung;
When, from their mountain holds, on the Moorish rout
      below,
Had rushed the Christians like a flood, and swept
      away the foe.
Awhile that melody is still, and then breaks forth anew
A wilder rhyme, a livelier note, of freedom and Peru.

For she has bound the sword to a youthful lover's
    side,
And sent him to the war the day she should have
    been his bride,
And bade him bear a faithful heart to battle for the
    right,
And held the fountains of her eyes till he was out of
    sight.
Since the parting kiss was given, six weary months
    are fled,
And yet the foe is in the land, and blood must yet be
    shed.

A white hand parts the branches, a lovely face looks
    forth,
And bright dark eyes gaze steadfastly and sadly to-
    ward the north.
Thou look'st in vain, sweet maiden, the sharpest sight
    would fail
To spy a sign of human life abroad in all the vale;
For the noon is coming on, and the sunbeams fiercely
    beat,
And the silent hills and forest-tops seem reeling in the
    heat.

That white hand is withdrawn, that fair sad face is
    gone,
But the music of that silver voice is flowing sweetly on,
Not as of late, in cheerful tones, but mournfully and
    low,—
A ballad of a tender maid heart-broken long ago,
Of him who died in battle, the youthful and the brave,
And her who died of sorrow, upon his early grave.

But see, along that mountain slope, a fiery horseman
    ride;
Mark his torn plume, his tarnished belt, the sabre at
    his side.

His spurs are buried rowel-deep, he rides with loosen-
    ed rein,
There's blood upon his charger's flank and foam upon
    the mane;
He speeds him toward the olive-grove, along that
    shaded hill:
God shield the helpless maiden there, if he should
    mean her ill!

And suddenly that song has ceased, and suddenly I
    hear
A shriek sent up amid the shade, a shriek—but not
    of fear.
For tender accents follow, and tenderer pauses speak
The overflow of gladness, when words are all too weak:
"I lay my good sword at thy feet, for now Peru is free,
And I am come to dwell beside the olive-grove with
    thee."

THE AFRICAN CHIEF.

Chained in the market-place he stood,
    A man of giant frame,
Amid the gathering multitude
    That shrunk to hear his name—
All stern of look and strong of limb,
    His dark eye on the ground:—
And silently they gazed on him,
    As on a lion bound.

Vainly, but well, that chief had fought,
    He was a captive now,
Yet pride, that fortune humbles not,
    Was written on his brow.

The scars his dark broad bosom wore,
　Showed warrior true and brave;
A prince among his tribe before,
　He could not be a slave.

Then to his conqueror he spake—
　"My brother is a king;
Undo this necklace from my neck,
　And take this bracelet ring,
And send me where my brother reigns,
　And I will fill thy hands
With store of ivory from the plains,
　And gold-dust from the sands."

"Not for thy ivory nor thy gold
　Will I unbind thy chain;
That bloody hand shall never hold
　The battle-spear again.
A price thy nation never gave
　Shall yet be paid for thee;
For thou shalt be the Christian's slave,
　In lands beyond the sea."

Then wept the warrior chief, and bade
　To shred his locks away;
And one by one, each heavy braid
　Before the victor lay.
Thick were the platted locks, and long,
　·And closely hidden there
Shone many a wedge of gold among
　The dark and crisped hair.

"Look, feast thy greedy eye with gold
　Long kept for sorest need:
Take it—thou askest sums untold,
　And say that I am freed.

Take it—my wife, the long, long day,
　　Weeps by the cocoa-tree,
And my young children leave their play,
　　And ask in vain for me."

" I take thy gold—but I have made
　　Thy fetters fast and strong,
And ween that by the cocoa shade
　　Thy wife will wait thee long."
Strong was the agony that shook
　　The captive's frame to hear,
And the proud meaning of his look
　　Was changed to mortal fear.

His heart was broken—crazed his brain:
　　At once his eye grew wild;
He struggled fiercely with his chain,
　　Whispered, and wept, and smiled;
Yet wore not long those fatal bands,
　　And once, at shut of day,
They drew him forth upon the sands,
　　The foul hyena's prey.

———— •••• ————

SPRING IN TOWN.

The country ever has a lagging Spring,
　　Waiting for May to call its violets forth,
And June its roses—showers and sunshine bring,
　　Slowly, the deepening verdure o'er the earth;
To put their foliage out, the woods are slack,
And one by one the singing-birds come back.

Within the city's bounds the time of flowers
   Comes earlier.   Let a mild and sunny day,
Such as full often, for a few bright hours,
   Breathes through the sky of March the airs of
      May,
Shine on our roofs and chase the wintry gloom—
And lo! our borders glow with sudden bloom.

For the wide sidewalks of Broadway are then
   Gorgeous as are a rivulet's banks in June,
That overhung with blossoms, through its glen,
   Slides soft away beneath the sunny noon,
And they who search the untrodden wood for flowers
Meet in its depths no lovelier ones than ours.

For here are eyes that shame the violet,
   Or the dark drop that on the pansy lies,
And foreheads, white, as when in clusters set,
   The anemones by forest mountains rise;·
And the spring-beauty boasts no tenderer streak
Than the soft red on many a youthful cheek.

And thick about those lovely temples lie
   Locks that the lucky Vignardonne has curled,
Thrice happy man! whose trade it is to buy,
   And bake, and braid those love-knots of the world;
Who curls of every glossy color keepest,
And sellest, it is said, the blackest cheapest.

And well thou mayst—for Italy's brown maids
   Send the dark locks with which their brows are
      dressed,
And Gascon lasses, from their jetty braids,
   Crop half, to buy a riband for the rest;
But the fresh Norman girls their tresses spare,
And the Dutch damsel keeps her flaxen hair.

Then, henceforth, let no maid nor matron grieve,
　To see her locks of an unlovely hue,
Frouzy or thin, for liberal art shall give
　Such piles of curls as nature never knew.
Eve, with her veil of tresses, at the sight
Had blushed, outdone, and owned herself a fright.

Soft voices and light laughter wake the street,
　Like notes of woodbirds, and where'er the eye
Threads the long way, plumes wave, and twinkling feet
　Fall light, as hastes that crowd of beauty by.
The ostrich, hurrying o'er the desert space,
Scarce bore those tossing plumes with fleeter pace.

No swimming Juno gait, of languor born,
　Is theirs, but a light step of freest grace,
Light as Camilla's o'er the unbent corn,—
　A step that speaks the spirit of the place,
Since Quiet, meek old dame, was driven away
To Sing Sing and the shores of Tappan bay.

Ye that dash by in chariots! who will care
　For steeds or footmen now? ye cannot show
Fair face, and dazzling dress, and graceful air,
　And last edition of the shape! Ah, no,
These sights are for the earth and open sky,
And your loud wheels unheeded rattle by.

------━◆◆◆━------

THE GLADNESS OF NATURE.

Is this a time to be cloudy and sad,
　When our mother Nature laughs around;
When even the deep blue heavens look glad,
　And gladness breathes from the blossoming ground!

There are notes of joy from the hang-bird and wren,
  And the gossip of swallows through all the sky;
The ground-squirrel gayly chirps by his den,
  And the wilding bee hums merrily by.

The clouds are at play in the azure space,
  And their shadows at play on the bright green vale,
And here they stretch to the frolic chase,
  And there they roll on the easy gale.

There's a dance of leaves in that aspen bower,
  There's a titter of winds in that beechen tree,
There's a smile on the fruit, and a smile on the flower,
  And a laugh from the brook that runs to the sea.

And look at the broad-faced sun, how he smiles
  On the dewy earth that smiles in his ray,
On the leaping waters and gay young isles;
  Ay, look, and he'll smile thy gloom away.

―――――・◆◆・―――――

THE DISINTERRED WARRIOR.

GATHER him to his grave again,
  And solemnly and softly lay,
Beneath the verdure of the plain,
  The warrior's scattered bones away.
Pay the deep reverence, taught of old,
  The homage of man's heart to death;
Nor dare to trifle with the mould
  Once hallowed by the Almighty's breath.

The soul hath quickened every part—
  That remnant of a martial brow,
Those ribs that held the mighty heart,
  That strong arm—strong no longer now.

Spare them, each mouldering relic spare,
  Of God's own image; let them rest,
Till not a trace shall speak of where
  The awful likeness was impressed.

For he was fresher from the hand
  That formed of earth the human face,
And to the elements did stand
  In nearer kindred than our race.
In many a flood to madness tossed,
  In many a storm has been his path;
He hid him not from heat or frost,
  But met them, and defied their wrath.

Then they were kind—the forests here,
  Rivers, and stiller waters, paid
A tribute to the net and spear
  Of the red ruler of the shade.
Fruits on the woodland branches lay,
  Roots in the shaded soil below,
The stars looked forth to teach his way,
  The still earth warned him of the foe.

A noble race! but they are gone,
  With their old forests wide and deep,
And we have built our homes upon
  Fields where their generations sleep.
Their fountains slake our thirst at noon,
  Upon their fields our harvest waves,
Our lovers woo beneath their moon—
  Then let us spare, at least, their graves!

MIDSUMMER.

A POWER is on the earth and in the air,
  From which the vital spirit shrinks afraid,
  And shelters him, in nooks of deepest shade,
From the hot steam and from the fiery glare.
Look forth upon the earth—her thousand plants
  Are smitten; even the dark sun-loving maize
  Faints in the field beneath the torrid blaze;
The herd beside the shaded fountain pants;
For life is driven from all the landscape brown;
  The bird has sought his tree, the snake his den,
  The trout floats dead in the hot stream, and men
Drop by the sun-stroke in the populous town:
  As if the Day of Fire had dawned, and sent
  Its deadly breath into the firmament.

------◆◆◆------

THE GREEK PARTISAN.

Our free flag is dancing
  In the free mountain air,
And burnished arms are glancing,
  And warriors gathering there;
And fearless is the little train
  Whose gallant bosoms shield it;
The blood that warms their hearts shall stain
  That banner, ere they yield it.

—Each dark eye is fixed on earth,
  And brief each solemn greeting;
There is no look nor sound of mirth,
  Where those stern men are meeting.

They go to the slaughter
  To strike the sudden blow,
And pour on earth, like water,
  The best blood of the foe;
To rush on them from rock and height,
  And clear the narrow valley,
Or fire their camp at dead of night,
  And fly before they rally.
—Chains are round our country pressed,
  And cowards have betrayed her,
And we must make her bleeding breast
  The grave of the invader.

Not till from her fetters
  We raise up Greece again,
And write, in bloody letters,
  That tyranny is slain,—
Oh, not till then the smile shall steal
  Across those darkened faces,
Nor one of all those warriors feel
  His children's dear embraces.
—Reap we not the ripened wheat,
  Till yonder hosts are flying,
And all their bravest, at our feet,
  Like autumn sheaves are lying.

THE TWO GRAVES.

'Tis a bleak wild hill, but green and bright
In the summer warmth and the mid-day light;
There's the hum of the bee and the chirp of the wren,
And the dash of the brook from the alder glen;
There's the sound of a bell from the scattered flock,
And the shade of the beech lies cool on the rock,
And fresh from the west is the free wind's breath,—
There is nothing here that speaks of death.

Far yonder, where orchards and gardens lie,
And dwellings cluster, 'tis there men die.
They are born, they die, and are buried near,
Where the populous grave-yard lightens the bier;
For strict and close are the ties that bind
In death the children of human-kind;
Yea, stricter and closer than those of life,—
'Tis a neighborhood that knows no strife.
They are noiselessly gathered—friend and foe—
To the still and dark assemblies below;
Without a frown or a smile they meet,
Each pale and calm in his winding-sheet;
In that sullen home of peace and gloom,
Crowded, like guests in a banquet-room.

Yet there are graves in this lonely spot,
Two humble graves,—but I meet them not.
I have seen them,—eighteen years are past,
Since I found their place in the brambles last,—
The place where, fifty winters ago,
An aged man in his locks of snow,
And an aged matron, withered with years,
Were solemnly laid!—but not with tears.

For none, who sat by the light of their hearth,
Beheld their coffins covered with earth;
Their kindred were far, and their children dead,
When the funeral prayer was coldly said.

Two low green hillocks, two small gray stones,
Rose over the place that held their bones;
But the grassy hillocks are levelled again,
And the keenest eye might search in vain,
'Mong briers, and ferns, and paths of sheep,
For the spot where the aged couple sleep

Yet well might they lay, beneath the soil
Of this lonely spot, that man of toil,
And trench the strong hard mould with the spade,
Where never before a grave was made;
For he hewed the dark old woods away,
And gave the virgin fields to the day;
And the gourd and the bean, beside his door,
Bloomed where their flowers ne'er opened before;
And the maize stood up, and the bearded rye
Bent low in the breath of an unknown sky.

'Tis said that when life is ended here,
The spirit is borne to a distant sphere;
That it visits its earthly home no more,
Nor looks on the haunts it loved before.
But why should the bodiless soul be sent
Far off, to a long, long banishment?
Talk not of the light and the living green!
It will pine for the dear familiar scene;
It will yearn, in that strange bright world, to behold
The rock and the stream it knew of old.

'Tis a cruel creed, believe it not!
Death to the good is a milder lot.
They are here,—they are here,—that harmless pair,
In the yellow sunshine and flowing air,

In the light cloud-shadows that slowly pass,
In the sounds that rise from the murmuring grass.
They sit where their humble cottage stood,
They walk by the waving edge of the wood,
And list to the long-accustomed flow
Of the brook that wets the rocks below.
Patient, and peaceful, and passionless,
As seasons on seasons swiftly press,
They watch, and wait, and linger around,
Till the day when their bodies shall leave the ground.

----•♦•----

THE CONJUNCTION OF JUPITER AND VENUS.

I would not always reason.   The straight path
Wearies us with its never-varying lines,
And we grow melancholy.   I would make
Reason my guide, but she should sometimes sit
Patiently by the way-side, while I traced
The mazes of the pleasant wilderness
Around me.   She should be my counsellor,
But not my tyrant.   For the spirit needs
Impulses from a deeper source than hers,
And there are motions, in the mind of man,
That she must look upon with awe.   I bow
Reverently to her dictates, but not less
Hold to the fair illusions of old time—
Illusions that shed brightness over life,
And glory over nature.   Look, even now,
Where two bright planets in the twilight meet,
Upon the saffron heaven,—the imperial star
Of Jove, and she that from her radiant urn
Pours forth the light of love.   Let me believe,
Awhile, that they are met for ends of good,

Amid the evening glory, to confer
Of men and their affairs, and to shed down
Kind influence. Lo! they brighten as we gaze,
And shake out softer fires! The great earth feel
The gladness and the quiet of the time.
Meekly the mighty river, that infolds
This mighty city, smooths his front, and far
Glitters and burns even to the rocky base
Of the dark heights that bound him to the west;
And a deep murmur, from the many streets,
Rises like a thanksgiving. Put we hence
Dark and sad thoughts awhile—there's time for them
Hereafter—on the morrow we will meet,
With melancholy looks, to tell our griefs,
And make each other wretched; this calm hour,
This balmy, blessed evening, we will give
To cheerful hopes and dreams of happy days,
Born of the meeting of those glorious stars.

Enough of drought has parched the year, and scared
The land with dread of famine. Autumn, yet,
Shall make men glad with unexpected fruits.
The dog-star shall shine harmless: genial days
Shall softly glide away into the keen
And wholesome cold of winter; he that fears
The pestilence, shall gaze on those pure beams,
And breathe, with confidence, the quiet air.

Emblems of power and beauty! well may they
Shine brightest on our borders, and withdraw
Towards the great Pacific, marking out
The path of empire. Thus, in our own land,
Ere long, the better Genius of our race,
Having encompassed earth, and tamed its tribes,
Shall sit him down beneath the farthest west,
By the shore of that calm ocean, and look back
On realms made happy.

　　　　　　　　　　Light the nuptial torch,
And say the glad, yet solemn rite, that knits
The youth and maiden.　Happy days to them
That wed this evening!—a long life of love,
And blooming sons and daughters!　Happy they
Born at this hour, for they shall see au age
Whiter and holier than the past, and go
Late to their graves.　Men shall wear softer hearts,
And shudder at the butcheries of war,
As now at other murders.

　　　　　　　　　　Hapless Greece!
Enough of blood has wet thy rocks, and stained
Thy rivers; deep enough thy chains have worn
Their links into thy flesh; the sacrifice
Of thy pure maidens, and thy innocent babes,
And reverend priests, has expiated all
Thy crimes of old.　In yonder mingling lights
There is au omen of good days for thee.
Thou shalt arise from midst the dust and sit
Again among the nations.　Thine own arm
Shall yet redeem thee.　Not in wars like thine
The world takes part.　Be it a strife of kings,—
Despot with despot battling for a throne,—
And Europe shall be stirred throughout her realms,
Nations shall put on harness, and shall fall
Upon each other, and in all their bounds
The wailing of the childless shall not cease.
Thine is a war for liberty, and thou
Must fight it single-handed.　The old world
Looks coldly on the murderers of thy race,
And leaves thee to the struggle; and the new,—
I fear me thou couldst tell a shameful tale
Of fraud and lust of gain;—thy treasury drained,
And Missolonghi fallen.　Yet thy wrongs
Shall put new strength into thy heart and hand,
And God and thy good sword shall yet work out,
For thee, a terrible deliverance.

A SUMMER RAMBLE.

THE quiet August noon has come,
  A slumberous silence fills the sky,
The fields are still, the woods are dumb,
  In glassy sleep the waters lie.

And mark yon soft white clouds that rest
  Above our vale, a moveless throng;
The cattle, on the mountain's breast,
  Enjoy the grateful shadow long.

Oh, how unlike those merry hours,
  In early June, when Earth laughs out,
When the fresh winds make love to flowers,
  And woodlands sing and waters shout.

When in the grass sweet voices talk,
  And strains of tiny music swell
From every moss-cup of the rock,
  From every nameless blossom's bell.

But now a joy too deep for sound,
  A peace no other season knows,
Hushes the heavens and wraps the ground,
  The blessing of supreme repose.

Away! I will not be, to-day,
  The only slave of toil and care.
Away from desk and dust! away!
  I'll be as idle as the air.

Beneath the open sky abroad,
　Among the plants and breathing things,
The sinless, peaceful works of God,
　I'll share the calm the season brings.

Come, thou, in whose soft eyes I see
　The gentle meanings of thy heart,
One day amid the woods with me,
　From men and all their cares apart.

And where, upon the meadow's breast,
　The shadow of the thicket lies,
The blue wild flowers thou gatherest
　Shall glow yet deeper near thine eyes.

Come, and when mid the calm profound,
　I turn, those gentle eyes to seek,
They, like the lovely landscape round,
　Of innocence and peace shall speak.

Rest here, beneath the unmoving shade,
　And on the silent valleys gaze,
Winding and widening, till they fade
　In you soft ring of summer haze.

The village trees their summits rear
　Still as its spire, and yonder flock
At rest in those calm fields appear
　As chiselled from the lifeless rock.

One tranquil mount the scene o'erlooks—
　There the hushed winds their sabbath keep,
While a near hum from bees and brooks
　Comes faintly like the breath of sleep.

Well may the gazer deem that when,
  Worn with the struggle and the strife,
And heart-sick at the wrongs of men,
  The good forsakes the scene of life;

Like this deep quiet that, awhile,
  Lingers the lovely landscape o'er,
Shall be the peace whose holy smile
  Welcomes him to a happier shore.

A SCENE ON THE BANKS OF THE HUDSON

Cool shades and dews are round my way,
And silence of the early day;
Mid the dark rocks that watch his bed,
Glitters the mighty Hudson spread,
Unrippled, save by drops that fall
From shrubs that fringe his mountain wall;
And o'er the clear still water swells
The music of the Sabbath bells.

All, save this little nook of land,
Circled with trees, on which I stand;
All, save that line of hills which lie
Suspended in the mimic sky—
Seems a blue void, above, below,
Through which the white clouds come and go;
And from the green world's farthest steep
I gaze into the airy deep.

Loveliest of lovely things are they,
On earth, that soonest pass away.
The rose that lives its little hour
Is prized beyond the sculptured flower,

Even love, long tried and cherished long,
Becomes more tender and more strong,
At thought of that insatiate grave
From which its yearnings cannot save.

River! in this still hour thou hast
Too much of heaven on earth to last;
Nor long may thy still waters lie,
An image of the glorious sky.
Thy fate and mine are not repose,
And ere another evening close,
Thou to thy tides shalt turn again,
And I to seek the crowd of men.

———— ❖❖ ————

THE HURRICANE.

Lord of the winds! I feel thee nigh,
I know thy breath in the burning sky!
And I wait, with a thrill in every vein,
For the coming of the hurricane!

And lo! on the wing of the heavy gales,
Through the boundless arch of heaven he sails,
Silent and slow, and terribly strong,
The mighty shadow is borne along,
Like the dark eternity to come;
While the world below, dismayed and dumb,
Through the calm of the thick hot atmosphere
Looks up at its gloomy folds with fear.

They darken fast; and the golden blaze
Of the sun is quenched in the lurid haze,
And he sends through the shade a funeral ray—
A glare that is neither night nor day,

A beam that touches, with hues of death,
The clouds above and the earth beneath.
To its covert glides the silent bird,
While the hurricane's distant voice is heard
Uplifted among the mountains round,
And the forests hear and answer the sound.

He is come! he is come! do ye not behold
His ample robes on the wind unrolled?
Giant of air! we bid thee hail!—
How his gray skirts toss in the whirling gale;
How his huge and writhing arms are bent,
To clasp the zone of the firmament,
And fold at length, in their dark embrace,
From mountain to mountain the visible space.

Darker—still darker! the whirlwinds bear
The dust of the plains to the middle air:
And hark to the crashing, long and loud,
Of the chariot of God in the thunder-cloud!
You may trace its path by the flashes that start
From the rapid wheels where'er they dart,
As the fire-bolts leap to the world below,
And flood the skies with a lurid glow.

What roar is that?—'tis the rain that breaks
In torrents away from the airy lakes,
Heavily poured on the shuddering ground,
And shedding a nameless horror round.
Ah! well-known woods, and mountains, and skies,
With the very clouds!—ye are lost to my eyes.
I seek ye vainly, and see in your place
The shadowy tempest that sweeps through space,
A whirling ocean that fills the wall
Of the crystal heaven, and buries all.
And I, cut off from the world, remain
Alone with the terrible hurricane.

WILLIAM TEIL

CHAINS may subdue the feeble spirit but thee,
　　TELL, of the iron heart! they could not tame!
　　For thou wert of the mountains; they proclaim
The everlasting creed of liberty.
That creed is written on the untrampled snow,
　　Thundered by torrents which no power can hold,
　　Save that of God, when he sends forth his cold,
And breathed by winds that through the free heaven
　　　　blow.
Thou, while thy prison walls were dark around,
　　Didst meditate the lesson Nature taught,
　　And to thy brief captivity was brought
A vision of thy Switzerland unbound.
　　The bitter cup they mingled, strengthened thee
　　For the great work to set thy country free.

———————●◆●———————

THE HUNTER'S SERENADE.

THY bower is finished, fairest!
　　Fit bower for hunter's bride—
Where old woods overshadow
　　The green savanna's side.

I've wandered long, and wandered far,
  And never have I met,
In all this lovely western land,
  A spot so lovely yet.
But I shall think it fairer,
  When thou art come to bless,
With thy sweet smile and silver voice,
  Its silent loveliness.

For thee the wild grape glistens,
  On sunny knoll and tree,
The slim papaya ripens
  Its yellow fruit for thee.
For thee the duck, on glassy stream,
  The prairie-fowl shall die,
My rifle for thy feast shall bring
  The wild swan from the sky.
The forest's leaping panther,
  Fierce, beautiful, and fleet,
Shall yield his spotted hide to be
  A carpet for thy feet.

I know, for thou hast told me,
  Thy maiden love of flowers;
Ah, those that deck thy gardens
  Are pale compared with ours.
When our wide woods and mighty lawns
  Bloom to the April skies,
The earth has no more gorgeous sight
  To show to human eyes.
In meadows red with blossoms,
  All summer long, the bee
Murmurs, and loads his yellow thighs,
  For thee, my love, and me.

Or wouldst thou gaze at tokens
  Of ages long ago—
Our old oaks stream with mosses,
  And sprout with mistletoe;
12

And mighty vines, like serpents, climb
   The giant sycamore;
And trunks, o'erthrown for centuries,
   Cumber the forest floor;
And in the great savanna,
   The solitary mound,
Built by the elder world, o'erlooks
   The loneliness around.

Come, thou hast not forgotten
   Thy pledge and promise quite,
With many blushes murmured,
   Beneath the evening light.
Come, the young violets crowd my door,
   Thy earliest look to win,
And at my silent window-sill
   The jessamine peeps in.
All day the red-bird warbles,
   Upon the mulberry near,
And the night-sparrow trills her song,
   All night, with none to hear.

THE GREEK BOY.

Gone are the glorious Greeks of old,
   Glorious in mien and mind;
Their bones are mingled with the mould,
   Their dust is on the wind;
The forms they hewed from living stone
Survive the waste of years, alone,
And, scattered with their ashes, show
What greatness perished long ago.

Yet fresh the myrtles there—the springs
 Gush brightly as of yore;
Flowers blossom from the dust of kings,
 As many an age before.
There nature moulds as nobly now,
As e'er of old, the human brow:
And copies still the martial form
That braved Platæa's battle storm.

Boy! thy first looks were taught to seek
 Their heaven in Hellas' skies;
Her airs have tinged thy dusky cheek,
 Her sunshine lit thine eyes;
Thine ears have drunk the woodland strains
Heard by old poets, and thy veins
Swell with the blood of demigods,
That slumber in thy country's sods.

Now is thy nation free—though late—
 Thy elder brethren broke—
Broke, ere thy spirit felt its weight,
 The intolerable yoke.
And Greece, decayed, dethroned, doth see
Her youth renewed in such as thee:
A shoot of that old vine that made
The nations silent in its shade.

THE PAST.

Thou unrelenting Past!
Strong are the barriers round thy dark domain,
 And fetters, sure and fast,
Hold all that enter thy unbreathing reign.

Far in thy realm withdrawn
Old empires sit in sullenness and gloom,
　And glorious ages gone
Lie deep within the shadow of thy womb.

Childhood, with all its mirth,
Youth, Manhood, Age that draws us to the ground,
　And last, Man's Life on earth,
Glide to thy dim dominions, and are bound.

Thou hast my better years,
Thou hast my earlier friends—the good—the kind,
　Yielded to thee with tears—
The venerable form—the exalted mind.

My spirit yearns to bring
The lost ones back—yearns with desire intense,
　And struggles hard to wring
Thy bolts apart, and pluck thy captives thence.

In vain—thy gates deny
All passage save to those who hence depart;
　Nor to the streaming eye
Thou giv'st them back—nor to the broken heart.

In thy abysses hide
Beauty and excellence unknown—to thee
　Earth's wonder and her pride
Are gathered, as the waters to the sea;

Labors of good to man,
Unpublished charity, unbroken faith,—
　Love, that midst grief began,
And grew with years, and faltered not in death.

Full many a mighty name
Lurks in thy depths, unuttered, unrevered;
 With thee are silent fame,
Forgotten arts, and wisdom disappeared.

 Thine for a space are they—
Yet shalt thou yield thy treasures up at last;
 Thy gates shall yet give way,
Thy bolts shall fall, inexorable Past!

 All that of good and fair
Has gone into thy womb from earliest time,
 Shall then come forth to wear
The glory and the beauty of its prime.

 They have not perished—no!
Kind words, remembered voices once so sweet,
 Smiles, radiant long ago,
And features, the great soul's apparent seat.

 All shall come back, each tie
Of pure affection shall be knit again;
 Alone shall Evil die,
And Sorrow dwell a prisoner in thy reign.

 And then shall I behold
Him, by whose kind paternal side I sprung,
 And her, who, still and cold,
Fills the next grave—the beautiful and young.

"UPON THE MOUNTAIN'S DISTANT HEAD"

Upon the mountain's distant head,
    With trackless snows for ever white,
Where all is still, and cold, and dead,
    Late shines the day's departing light.

But far below those icy rocks,
    The vales, in summer bloom arrayed,
Woods full of birds, and fields of flocks,
    Are dim with mist and dark with shade.

'Tis thus, from warm and kindly hearts,
    And eyes where generous meanings burn,
Earliest the light of life departs,
    But lingers with the cold and stern.

THE EVENING WIND.

Spirit that breathest through my lattice, thou
    That cool'st the twilight of the sultry day,
Gratefully flows thy freshness round my brow:
    Thou hast been out upon the deep at play,
Riding all day the wild blue waves till now,
    Roughening their crests, and scattering high their
        spray
And swelling the white sail.   I welcome thee
To the scorched land, thou wanderer of the sea!

Nor I alone—a thousand bosoms round
  Inhale thee in the fulness of delight;
And languid forms rise up, and pulses bound
  Livelier, at coming of the wind of night;
And, languishing to hear thy grateful sound,
  Lies the vast inland stretched beyond the sight.
Go forth into the gathering shade; go forth,
God's blessing breathed upon the fainting earth!

Go, rock the little wood-bird in his nest,
  Curl the still waters, bright with stars, and rouse
The wide old wood from his majestic rest,
  Summoning from the innumerable boughs
The strange, deep harmonies that haunt his breast:
  Pleasant shall be thy way where meekly bows
The shutting flower, and darkling waters pass,
And where the o'ershadowing branches sweep the
    grass.

The faint old man shall lean his silver head
  To feel thee; thou shalt kiss the child asleep,
And dry the moistened curls that overspread
  His temples, while his breathing grows more deep:
And they who stand about the sick man's bed,
  Shall joy to listen to thy distant sweep,
And softly part his curtains to allow
Thy visit, grateful to his burning brow.

Go—but the circle of eternal change,
  Which is the life of nature, shall restore,
With sounds and scents from all thy mighty range,
  Thee to thy birthplace of the deep once more;
Sweet odors in the sea-air, sweet and strange,
  Shall tell the home-sick mariner of the shore;
And, listening to thy murmur, he shall deem
He hears the rustling leaf and running stream.

"WHEN THE FIRMAMENT QUIVERS WITH DAYLIGHT'S YOUNG BEAM."

WHEN the firmament quivers with daylight's young
    beam,
  And the woodlands awaking burst into a hymn,
And the glow of the sky blazes back from the stream,
  How the bright ones of heaven in the brightness
    grow dim.

Oh! 'tis sad, in that moment of glory and song,
  To see, while the hill-tops are waiting the sun,
The glittering band that kept watch all night long
  O'er Love and o'er Slumber, go out one by one:

Till the circle of ether, deep, ruddy, and vast,
  Scarce glimmers with one of the train that were
    there;
And their leader the day-star, the brightest and last,
  Twinkles faintly and fades in that desert of air.

Thus, Oblivion, from midst of whose shadow we came,
  Steals o'er us again when life's twilight is gone;
And the crowd of bright names, in the heaven of fame
  Grow pale and are quenched as the years hasten on.

Let them fade—but we'll pray that the age, in whose
    flight,
  Of ourselves and our friends the remembrance shall
    die,
May rise o'er the world, with the gladness and light
  Of the morning that withers the stars from the sky.

"INNOCENT CHILD AND SNOW-WHITE FLOWER."

INNOCENT child and snow-white flower!
Well are ye paired in your opening hour.
Thus should the pure and the lovely meet,
Stainless with stainless, and sweet with sweet.

White as those leaves, just blown apart,
Are the folds of thy own young heart,
Guilty passion and cankering care
Never have left their traces there.

Artless one! though thou gazest now
O'er the white blossom with earnest brow,
Soon will it tire thy childish eye;
Fair as it is, thou wilt throw it by.

Throw it aside in thy weary hour,
Throw to the ground the fair white flower;
Yet, as thy tender years depart,
Keep that white and innocent heart.

TO THE RIVER ARVE.

SUPPOSED TO BE WRITTEN AT A HAMLET NEAR THE FOO
OF MONT BLANC.

Not from the sands or cloven rocks,
   Thou rapid Arve! thy waters flow;
Nor earth, within her bosom, locks
   Thy dark unfathomed wells below.
Thy springs are in the cloud, thy stream
   Begins to move and murmur first
Where ice-peaks feel the noonday beam,
   Or rain-storms on the glacier burst.

Born where the thunder and the blast
   And morning's earliest light are born,
Thou rushest swoln, and loud, and fast,
   By these low homes, as if in scorn :
Yet humbler springs yield purer waves;
   And brighter, glassier streams than thine,
Sent up from earth's unlighted caves,
   With heaven's own beam and image shine.

Yet stay; for here are flowers and trees;
   Warm rays on cottage roofs are here,
And laugh of girls, and hum of bees—
   Here linger till thy waves are clear.
Thou heedest not—thou hastest on ;
   From steep to steep thy torrent falls,
Till, mingling with the mighty Rhone,
   It rests beneath Geneva's walls.

Rush on—but were there one with me
    That loved me, I would light my hearth
Here, where with God's own majesty
    Are touched the features of the earth.
By these old peaks, white, high, and vast,
    Still rising as the tempests beat,
Here would I dwell, and sleep, at last,
    Among the blossoms at their feet.

TO COLE, THE PAINTER, DEPARTING FOR EUROPE.

A SONNET.

THINE eyes shall see the light of distant skies:
    Yet, COLE! thy heart shall bear to Europe's strand
    A living image of our own bright land,
Such as upon thy glorious canvas lies;
Lone lakes—savannas where the bison roves—
    Rocks rich with summer garlands — solemn
        streams—
    Skies, where the desert eagle wheels and screams—
Spring bloom and autumn blaze of boundless groves.
Fair scenes shall greet thee where thou goest—fair,
    But different—every where the trace of men,
    Paths, homes, graves, ruins, from the lowest glen
To where life shrinks from the fierce Alpine air,
    Gaze on them, till the tears shall dim thy sight,
    But keep that earlier, wilder image bright.

TO THE FRINGED GENTIAN

Thou blossom bright with autumn dew,
And colored with the heaven's own blue,
That openest when the quiet light
Succeeds the keen and frosty night.

Thou comest not when violets lean
O'er wandering brooks and springs unseen,
Or columbines, in purple dressed,
Nod o'er the ground-bird's hidden nest.

Thou waitest late and com'st alone,
When woods are bare and birds are flown,
And frosts and shortening days portend
The aged year is near his end.

Then doth thy sweet and quiet eye
Look through its fringes to the sky,
Blue—blue—as if that sky let fall
A flower from its ceruleau wall.

I would that thus, when I shall see
The hour of death draw near to me,
Hope, blossoming within my heart,
May look to heaven as I depart.

THE TWENTY-SECOND OF DECEMBER.

WILD was the day; the wintry sea
　Moaned sadly on New England's strand,
When first the thoughtful and the free,
　Our fathers, trod the desert land.

They little thought how pure a light,
　With years, should gather round that day;
How love should keep their memories bright,
　How wide a realm their sons should sway.

Green are their bays; but greener still
　Shall round their spreading fame be wreathed,
And regions, now untrod, shall thrill
　With reverence when their names are breathed.

Till where the sun, with softer fires,
　Looks on the vast Pacific's sleep,
The children of the pilgrim sires
　This hallowed day like us shall keep.

HYMN TO THE CITY.

　Nor in the solitude
Alone may man commune with Heaven, or see
　　Only in savage wood
And sunny vale, the present Deity;
　　Or only hear his voice
Where the winds whisper and the waves rejoice.

Even here do I behold
Thy steps, Almighty!—here, amidst the crowd,
    Through the great city rolled,
With everlasting murmur deep and loud—
    Choking the ways that wind
'Mongst the proud piles, the work of human kind.

Thy golden sunshine comes
From the round heaven, and on their dwellings lies,
    And lights their inner homes;
For them thou fill'st with air the unbounded skies,
    And givest them the stores
Of ocean, and the harvests of its shores.

Thy Spirit is around,
Quickening the restless mass that sweeps along;
    And this eternal sound—
Voices and footfalls of the numberless throng—
    Like the resounding sea,
Or like the rainy tempest, speaks of thee.

And when the hours of rest
Come, like a calm upon the mid-sea brine,
    Hushing its billowy breast—
The quiet of that moment too is thine;
    It breathes of Him who keeps
The vast and helpless city while it sleeps.

THE PRAIRIES.

THESE are the gardens of the Desert, these
The unshorn fields, boundless and beautiful,
For which the speech of England has no name—
The Prairies. I behold them for the first,
And my heart swells, while the dilated sight
Takes in the encircling vastness. Lo! they stretch
In airy undulations, far away,
As if the ocean, in his gentlest swell,
Stood still, with all his rounded billows fixed,
And motionless for ever.—Motionless?—
No—they are all unchained again. The clouds
Sweep over with their shadows, and, beneath,
The surface rolls and fluctuates to the eye;
Dark hollows seem to glide along and chase
The sunny ridges. Breezes of the South!
Who toss the golden and the flame-like flowers,
And pass the prairie-hawk that, poised on high,
Flaps his broad wings, yet moves not—ye have played
Among the palms of Mexico and vines
Of Texas, and have crisped the limpid brooks
That from the fountains of Sonora glide
Into the calm Pacific—have ye fanned
A nobler or a lovelier scene than this?
Man hath no part in all this glorious work:
The hand that built the firmament hath heaved
And smoothed these verdant swells, and sown their
    slopes
With herbage, planted them with island groves,
And hedged them round with forests. Fitting floor
For this magnificent temple of the sky—
With flowers whose glory and whose multitude·
Rival the constellations! The great heavens

Seem to stoop down upon the scene in love,—
A nearer vault, and of a tenderer blue,
Than that which bends above our eastern hills.

    As o'er the verdant waste I guide my steed,
Among the high rank grass that sweeps his sides
The hollow beating of his footstep seems
A sacrilegious sound.   I think of those
Upon whose rest he tramples.   Are they here—
The dead of other days?—and did the dust
Of these fair solitudes once stir with life
And burn with passion?   Let the mighty mounds
That overlook the rivers, or that rise
In the dim forest crowded with old oaks,
Answer.   A race, that long has passed away,
Built them;—a disciplined and populous race
Heaped with long toil, the earth, while yet the Greek
Was hewing the Pentelicus to forms
Of symmetry, and rearing on its rock
The glittering Parthenon.   These ample fields
Nourished their harvests, here their herds were fed,
When haply by their stalls the bison lowed,
And bowed his maned shoulder to the yoke.
All day this desert murmured with their toils,
Till twilight blushed, and lovers walked, and wooed
In a forgotten language, and old tunes,
From instruments of unremembered form,
Gave the soft winds a voice.   The red man came—
The roaming hunter tribes, warlike and fierce,
And the mound-builders vanished from the earth.
The solitude of centuries untold
Has settled where they dwelt.   The prairie-wolf
Hunts in their meadows, and his fresh-dug den
Yawns by my path.   The gopher mines the ground
Where stood their swarming cities.   All is gone;
All—save the piles of earth that hold their bones,
The platforms where they worshipped unknown gods,
The barriers which they builded from the soil

To keep the foe at bay—till o'er the walls
The wild beleaguerers broke, and, one by one,
The strongholds of the plain were forced, and heaped
With corpses. The brown vultures of the wood
Flocked to those vast uncovered sepulchres,
And sat, unscared and silent, at their feast.
Haply some solitary fugitive,
Lurking in marsh and forest, till the sense
Of desolation and of fear became
Bitterer than death, yielded himself to die.
Man's better nature triumphed then. Kind word
Welcomed and soothed him; the rude conquerors
Seated the captive with their chiefs; he chose
A bride among their maidens, and at length
Seemed to forget,—yet ne'er forgot,—the wife
Of his first love, and her sweet little ones,
Butchered, amid their shrieks, with all his race.

Thus change the forms of being. Thus arise
Races of living things, glorious in strength,
And perish, as the quickening breath of God
Fills them, or is withdrawn. The red man, too,
Has left the blooming wilds he ranged so long,
And, nearer to the Rocky Mountains, sought
A wilder hunting-ground. The beaver builds
No longer by these streams, but far away,
On waters whose blue surface ne'er gave back
The white man's face—among Missouri's springs,
And pools whose issues swell the Oregan,
He rears his little Venice. In these plains
The bison feeds no more. Twice twenty leagues
Beyond remotest smoke of hunter's camp,
Roams the majestic brute, in herds that shake
The earth with thundering steps—yet here I meet
His ancient footprints stamped beside the pool.

Still this great solitude is quick with life.
Myriads of insects, gaudy as the flowers

They flutter over, gentle quadrupeds,
And birds, that scarce have learned the fear of man,
Are here, and sliding reptiles of the ground,
Startlingly beautiful. The graceful deer
Bounds to the wood at my approach. The bee,
A more adventurous colonist than man,
With whom he came across the eastern deep,
Fills the savannas with his murmurings,
And hides his sweets, as in the golden age,
Within the hollow oak. I listen long
To his domestic hum, and think I hear
The sound of that advancing multitude
Which soon shall fill these deserts. From the ground
Comes up the laugh of children, the soft voice
Of maidens, and the sweet and solemn hymn
Of Sabbath worshippers. The low of herds
Blends with the rustling of the heavy grain
Over the dark-brown furrows. All at once
A fresher wind sweeps by, and breaks my dream,
And I am in the wilderness alone.

SONG OF MARION'S MEN.

Our band is few, but true and tried,
   Our leader frank and bold;
The British soldier trembles
   When Marion's name is told.
Our fortress is the good greenwood,
   Our tent the cypress-tree;
We know the forest round us,
   As seamen know the sea.

We know its walls of thorny vines,
  Its glades of reedy grass,
Its safe and silent islands
  Within the dark morass.

Wo to the English soldiery
  That little dread us near !
On them shall light at midnight
  A strange and sudden fear :
When, waking to their tents on fire,
  They grasp their arms in vain,
And they who stand to face us
  Are beat to earth again ;
And they who fly in terror deem
  A mighty host behind,
And hear the tramp of thousands
  Upon the hollow wind.

Then sweet the hour that brings release
  From danger and from toil :
We talk the battle over,
  And share the battle's spoil.
The woodland rings with laugh and shout,
  As if a hunt were up,
And woodland flowers are gathered
  To crown the soldier's cup.
With merry songs we mock the wind
  That in the pine-top grieves,
And slumber long and sweetly
  On beds of oaken leaves.

Well knows the fair and friendly moon
  The band that Marion leads—
The glitter of their rifles,
  The scampering of their steeds.
'Tis life to guide the fiery barb
  Across the moonlight plain ;
'Tis life to feel the night-wind
  That lifts his tossing mane.

A moment in the British camp—
  A moment—and away
Back to the pathless forest,
  Before the peep of day.

Grave men there are by broad Santee,
  Grave men with hoary hairs,
Their hearts are all with Marion,
  For Marion are their prayers.
And lovely ladies greet our band
  With kindliest welcoming,
With smiles like those of summer,
  And tears like those of spring.
For them we wear these trusty arms,
  And lay them down no more
Till we have driven the Briton,
  For ever, from our shore.

THE ARCTIC LOVER.

Gone is the long, long winter night;
  Look, my beloved one!
How glorious, through his depths of light,
  Rolls the majestic sun!
The willows, waked from winter's death,
Give out a fragrance like thy breath—
  The summer is begun!

Ay, 'tis the long bright summer day:
  Hark, to that mighty crash!
The loosened ice-ridge breaks away—
  The smitten waters flash.

Seaward the glittering mountain rides,
While, down its green translucent sides,
　The foamy torrents dash.

See, love, my boat is moored for thee,
　By ocean's weedy floor—
The petrel does not skim the sea
　More swiftly than my oar.
We'll go, where, on the rocky isles,
Her eggs the screaming sea-fowl piles
　Beside the pebbly shore.

Or, bide thou where the poppy blows,
　With wind-flowers frail and fair,
While I, upon this isle of snows,
　Seek and defy the bear.
Fierce though he be, and huge of frame,
This arm his savage strength shall tame,
　And drag him from his lair.

When crimson sky and flamy cloud
　Bespeak the summer o'er,
And the dead valleys wear a shroud
　Of snows that melt no more,
I'll build of ice thy winter home,
With glistening walls and glassy dome,
　And spread with skins the floor.

The white fox by thy couch shall play;
　And, from the frozen skies,
The meteors of a mimic day
　Shall flash upon thine eyes.
And I—for such thy vow—meanwhile
Shall hear thy voice and see thy smile,
　Till that long midnight flies.

THE JOURNEY OF LIFE.

BENEATH the waning moon I walk at night,
    And muse on human life—for all around
Are dim uncertain shapes that cheat the sight,
    And pitfalls lurk in shade along the ground,
And broken gleams of brightness, here and there,
Glance through, and leave unwarmed the death-like air.

The trampled earth returns a sound of fear—
    A hollow sound, as if I walked on tombs;
And lights, that tell of cheerful homes, appear
    Far off, and die like hope amid the glooms.
A mournful wind across the landscape flies,
And the wide atmosphere is full of sighs.

And I, with faltering footsteps, journey on,
    Watching the stars that roll the hours away,
Till the faint light that guides me now is gone,
    And, like another life, the glorious day
Shall open o'er me from the empyreal height,
With warmth, and certainty, and boundless light.

TRANSLATIONS.

VERSION OF A FRAGMENT OF SIMONIDES.

The night winds howled—the billows dashed
    Against the tossing chest;
As Danaë to her broken heart
    Her slumbering infant pressed.

" My little child "—in tears she said—
    " To wake and weep is mine,
But thou canst sleep—thou dost not know
    Thy mother's lot, and thine.

" The moon is up, the moonbeams smile—
    They tremble on the main;
But dark, within my floating cell,
    To me they smile in vain.

" Thy folded mantle wraps thee warm,
    Thy clustering locks are dry,
Thou dost not hear the shrieking gust,
    Nor breakers booming high.

" As o'er thy sweet unconscious face
   A mournful watch I keep,
I think, didst thou but know thy fate,
   How thou wouldst also weep.

" Yet, dear one, sleep, and sleep, ye winds
   That vex the restless brine—
When shall these eyes, my babe, be sealed
   As peacefully as thine ! "

FROM THE SPANISH OF VILLEGAS.

'Tis sweet, in the green Spring,
To gaze upon the wakening fields around ;
   Birds in the thicket sing,
Winds whisper, waters prattle from the ground ;
   A thousand odors rise,
Breathed up from blossoms of a thousand dyes.

   Shadowy, and close, and cool,
The pine and poplar keep their quiet nook ;
   For ever fresh and full,
Shines, at their feet, the thirst-inviting brook ;
   And the soft herbage seems
Spread for a place of banquets and of dreams.

   Thou, who alone art fair,
And whom alone I love, art far away.
   Unless thy smile be there,
It makes me sad to see the earth so gay ;
   I care not if the train
Of leaves, and flowers, and zephyrs go again.

MARY MAGDALEN.

FROM THE SPANISH OF BARTOLOME LEONARDO DE ARGENSOLA.

BLESSED, yet sinful one, and broken-hearted !
   The crowd are pointing at the thing forlorn,
     In wonder and in scorn !
Thou weepest days of innocence departed ;
   Thou weepest, and thy tears have power to move
     The Lord to pity and love.

The greatest of thy follies is forgiven,
   Even for the least of all the tears that shine
     On that pale cheek of thine.
Thou didst kneel down, to Him who came from heaven,
   Evil and ignorant, and thou shalt rise
     Holy, and pure, and wise.

It is not much that to the fragrant blossom
   The ragged brier should change ; the bitter fir,
     Distil Arabian myrrh !
Nor that, upon the wintry desert's bosom,
   The harvest should rise plenteous, and the swain
     Bear home the abundant grain.

But come and see the bleak and barren mountains
   Thick to their tops with roses : come and see
     Leaves on the dry dead tree :
The perished plant, set out by living fountains,
   Grows fruitful, and its beauteous branches rise,
     For ever, towards the skies.

14

.

THE LIFE OF THE BLESSED.

FROM THE SPANISH OF LUIS PONCE DE LEON.

REGION of life and light !
Land of the good whose earthly toils are o'er !
  Nor frost nor heat may blight
  Thy vernal beauty, fertile shore,
Yielding thy blessed fruits for evermore.

  There, without crook or sling,
Walks the good shepherd; blossoms white and red
  Round his meek temples cling;
  And to sweet pastures led,
His own loved flock beneath his eye is fed.

  He guides, and near him they
Follow delighted, for he makes them go
  Where dwells eternal May,
  And heavenly roses blow,
Deathless, and gathered but again to grow.

  He leads them to the height
Named of the infinite and long-sought Good,
  And fountains of delight;
  And where his feet have stood
Springs up, along the way, their tender food.

  And when, in the mid skies,
The climbing sun has reached his highest bound,
  Reposing as he lies,
  With all his flock around,   .
He witches the still air with numerous sound.

From his sweet lute flow forth
Immortal harmonies, of power to still
    All passions born of earth,
    And draw the ardent will
Its destiny of goodness to fulfil.

    Might but a little part,
A wandering breath of that high melody,
    Descend into my heart,
    And change it till it be
Transformed and swallowed up, oh love, in thee.

    Ah! then my soul should know,
Beloved! where thou liest at noon of day,
    And from this place of woe
    Released, should take its way
To mingle with thy flock and never stray.

FATIMA AND RADUAN.

FROM THE SPANISH.

Diamante falso y fingido,
Engastado en pedernal, &c.

"FALSE diamond set in flint! hard heart in haughty
    breast!
By a softer, warmer bosom the tiger's couch is prest.
Thou art fickle as the sea, thou art wandering as the
    wind,
And the restless ever-mounting flame is not more hard
    to bind.

If the tears I shed were tongues, yet all too few
    would be
To tell of all the treachery that thou hast shown to me.
Oh! I could chide thee sharply—but every maiden
    knows
That she who chides her lover, forgives him ere he goes.

"Thou hast called me oft the flower of all Grenada's
    maids,
Thou hast said that by the side of me the first and
    fairest fades;
And they thought thy heart was mine, and it seemed
    to every one
That what thou didst to win my love, for love of
    me was done.
Alas! if they but knew thee, as mine it is to know,
They well might see another mark to which thine ar-
    rows go;
But thou giv'st me little heed—for I speak to one who
    knows
That she who chides her lover, forgives him ere he
    goes.

"It wearies me, mine enemy, that I must weep and
    bear
What fills thy heart with triumph, and fills my own
    with care.
Thou art leagued with those that hate me, and ah!
    thou know'st I feel
That cruel words as surely kill as sharpest blades of
    steel.
'Twas the doubt that thou wert false that wrung my
    heart with pain;
But, now I know thy perfidy, I shall be well again.
I would proclaim thee as thou art—but every maiden
    knows
That she who chides her lover, forgives him ere he
    goes."

Thus Fatima complained to the valiant Raduan,
Where underneath the myrtles Alhambra's fountains
    ran:
The Moor was inly moved, and blameless as he was,
He took her white hand in his own, and pleaded thus
    his cause:
"Oh, lady, dry those star-like eyes—their dimness
    does me wrong;
If my heart be made of flint, at least 'twill keep thy
    image long;
Thou hast uttered cruel words—but I grieve the less
    for those,
Since she who chides her lover, forgives him ere he
    goes."

LOVE AND FOLLY.

FROM LA FONTAINE.

Love's worshippers alone can know
    The thousand mysteries that are his;
His blazing torch, his twanging bow,
    His blooming age are mysteries.
A charming science—but the day
    Were all too short to con it o'er;
So take of me this little lay,
    A sample of its boundless lore.

As once, beneath the fragrant shade
    Of myrtles fresh in heaven's pure air,
The children, Love and Folly, played—
    A quarrel rose betwixt the pair.

Love said the gods should do him right—
    But Folly vowed to do it then,
And struck him, o'er the orbs of sight,
    So hard he never saw again.

His lovely mother's grief was deep
    She called for vengeance on the deed;
A beauty does not vainly weep,
    Nor coldly does a mother plead.
A shade came o'er the eternal bliss
    That fills the dwellers of the skies;
Even stony-hearted Nemesis,
    And Rhadamanthus, wiped their eyes.

"Behold," she said, "this lovely boy,"
    While streamed afresh her graceful tears,
"Immortal, yet shut out from joy
    And sunshine, all his future years.
The child can never take, you see,
    A single step without a staff—
The harshest punishment would be
    Too lenient for the crime by half."

All said that Love had suffered wrong,
    And well that wrong should be repaid;
Then weighed the public interest long,
    And long the party's interest weighed.
And thus decreed the court above—
    "Since Love is blind from Folly's blow,
Let Folly be the guide of Love,
    Where'er the boy may choose to go."

THE SIESTA.

FROM THE SPANISH.

Vientecico murmurador,
Que lo gozas y andas todo, &c.

Airs, that wander and murmur round,
　　Bearing delight where'er ye blow!
Make in the elms a lulling sound,
　　While my lady sleeps in the shade below.

Lighten and lengthen her noonday rest,
　　Till the heat of the noonday sun is o'er.
Sweet be her slumbers! though in my breast
　　The pain she has waked may slumber no more.
Breathing soft from the blue profound,
　　Bearing delight where'er ye blow,
Make in the elms a lulling sound,
　　While my lady sleeps in the shade below.

Airs! that over the bending boughs,
　　And under the shade of pendent leaves,
Murmur soft, like my timid vows
　　Or the secret sighs my bosom heaves,—
Gently sweeping the grassy ground,
　　Bearing delight where'er ye blow,
Make in the elms a lulling sound,
　　While my lady sleeps in the shade below.

THE ALCAYDE OF MOLINA.

FROM THE SPANISH.

To the town of Atienza, Molina's brave Alcayde,
The courteous and the valorous, led forth his bold
    brigade.
The Moor came back in triumph, he came without a
    wound,
With many a Christian standard, and Christian cap-
    tive bound.
He passed the city portals, with swelling heart and
    vain,
And towards his lady's dwelling he rode with slack-
    ened rein ;
Two circuits on his charger he took, and at the third,
From the door of her balcony Zelinda's voice was
    heard.
"Now if thou wert not shameless," said the lady to
    the Moor,
"Thou wouldst neither pass my dwelling, nor stop
    before my door.
Alas for poor Zelinda, and for her wayward mood,
That one in love with peace should have loved a man
    of blood !
Since not that thou wert noble I chose thee for my
    knight,
But that thy sword was dreaded in tournay and in
    fight.
Ah, thoughtless and unhappy ! that I should fail to see
How ill the stubborn flint and the yielding wax agree.
Boast not thy love for me, while the shrieking of the fife
Can change thy mood of mildness to fury and to strife.

Say not my voice is magic—thy pleasure is to hear
The bursting of the carbine, and shivering of the spear
Well, follow thou thy choice—to the battle-field away,
To thy triumphs and thy trophies, since I am less than
    they.
Thrust thy arm into thy buckler, gird on thy crooked
    brand,
And call upon thy trusty squire to bring thy spears
    in hand.
Lead forth thy band to skirmish, by mountain and by
    mead,
On thy dappled Moorish barb, or thy fleeter border
    steed.
Go, waste the Christian hamlets, and sweep away
    their flocks,
From Almazan's broad meadows to Siguenza's rocks.
Leave Zelinda altogether, whom thou leavest oft and
    long,
And in the life thou lovest, forget whom thou dost
    wrong.
These eyes shall not recall thee, though they meet no
    more thine own,
Though they weep that thou art absent, and that I
    am all alone."
She ceased, and turning from him her flushed and an-
    gry cheek,
Shut the door of her balcony before the Moor could
    speak.

THE DEATH OF ALIATAR.

FROM THE SPANISH.

'Tis not with gilded sabres
 That gleam in baldricks blue,
Nor nodding plumes in caps of Fez,
 Of gay and gaudy hue—
But, habited in mourning weeds,
 Come marching from afar,
By four and four, the valiant men
 Who fought with Aliatar.
All mournfully and slowly
 The afflicted warriors come,
To the deep wail of the trumpet,
 And beat of muffled drum.

The banner of the Phenix,
 The flag that loved the sky,
That scarce the wind dared wanton with,
 It flew so proud and high—
Now leaves its place in battle-field,
 And sweeps the ground in grief,
The bearer drags its glorious folds
 Behind the fallen chief,
As mournfully and slowly
 The afflicted warriors come,
To the deep wail of the trumpet,
 And beat of muffled drum.

Brave Aliatar led forward
 A hundred Moors to go
To where his brother held Motril
 Against the leaguering foe.

On horseback went the gallant Moor,
  That gallant band to lead;
And now his bier is at the gate,
  From which he pricked his steed.
While mournfully and slowly
  The afflicted warriors come,
To the deep wail of the trumpet,
  And beat of muffled drum.

The knights of the Grand Master
  In crowded ambush lay;
They rushed upon him where the reeds
  Were thick beside the way;
They smote the valiant Aliatar,
  They smote the warrior dead,
And broken, but not beaten, were
  The gallant ranks he led.
Now mournfully and slowly
  The afflicted warriors come,
To the deep wail of the trumpet,
  And beat of muffled drum.

Oh! what was Zayda's sorrow,
  How passionate her cries!
Her lover's wounds streamed not more free,
  Than that poor maiden's eyes.
Say, Love—for didst thou see her tears:
  Oh, no! he drew more tight
The blinding fillet o'er his lids
  To spare his eyes the sight.
While mournfully and slowly
  The afflicted warriors come,
To the deep wail of the trumpet,
  And beat of muffled drum.

Nor Zayda weeps him only,
  But all that dwell between
The great Alhambra's palace walls
  And springs of Albaicin.

The ladies weep the flower of knights,
The brave the bravest here;
The people weep a champion,
The Alcaydes a noble peer.
While mournfully and slowly
The afflicted warriors come,
To the deep wail of the trumpet,
And beat of muffled drum.

LOVE IN THE AGE OF CHIVALRY.

FROM PEYRE VIDAL, THE TROUBADOUR.

THE earth was sown with early flowers,
The heavens were blue and bright—
I met a youthful cavalier
As lovely as the light.
I knew him not—but in my heart
His graceful image lies,
And well I marked his open brow,
His sweet and tender eyes,
His ruddy lips that ever smiled,
His glittering teeth betwixt,
And flowing robe embroidered o'er,
With leaves and blossoms mixed.
He wore a chaplet of the rose;
His palfrey, white and sleek,
Was marked with many an ebon spot,
And many a purple streak;
Of jasper was his saddle-bow,
His housings sapphire stone,
And brightly in his stirrup glanced
The purple calcedon.

Fast rode the gallant cavalier,
  As youthful horsemen ride;
"Peyre Vidal! know that I am Love,"
  The blooming stranger cried;
"And this is Mercy by my side,
  A dame of high degree;
This maid is Chastity," he said,
  "This squire is Loyalty."

————•••————

THE LOVE OF GOD.

FROM THE PROVENÇAL OF BERNARD RASCAS.

ALL things that are on earth shall wholly pass away,
Except the love of God, which shall live and last for
  aye.
The forms of men shall be as they had never been;
The blasted groves shall lose their fresh and tender
  green;
The birds of the thicket shall end their pleasant song,
And the nightingale shall cease to chant the evening
  long.
The kine of the pasture shall feel the dart that kills,
And all the fair white flocks shall perish from the hills.
The goat and antlered stag, the wolf and the fox,
The wild boar of the wood, and the chamois of the
  rocks,
And the strong and fearless bear, in the trodden dust
  shall lie;
And the dolphin of the sea, and the mighty whale,
  shall die.

15

And realms shall be dissolved, and empires be no more,
And they shall bow to death, who ruled from shore
    to shore;
And the great globe itself, so the holy writings tell,
With the rolling firmament, where the starry armies
    dwell,
Shall melt with fervent heat—they shall all pass away,
Except the love of God, which shall live and last for
    aye.

———————•◆•———————

FROM THE SPANISH OF PEDRO DE CASTRO Y AÑAYA.

STAY, rivulet, nor haste to leave
    The lovely vale that lies around thee.
Why wouldst thou be a sea at eve,
    When but a fount the morning found thee?

Born when the skies began to glow,
    Humblest of all the rock's cold daughters,
No blossom bowed its stalk to show
    Where stole thy still and scanty waters.

Now on thy stream the noonbeams look,
    Usurping, as thou downward driftest,
Its crystal from the clearest brook,
    Its rushing current from the swiftest.

Ah! what wild haste!—and all to be
    A river and expire in ocean.
Each fountain's tribute hurries thee
    To that vast grave with quicker motion.

Far better 'twere to linger still
   In this green vale, these flowers to cherish,
And die in peace, an aged rill,
   Than thus, a youthful Danube, perish.

SONNET.

FROM THE PORTUGUESE OF SEMEDO.

It is a fearful night; a feeble glare
   Streams from the sick moon in the o'erclouded sky;
   The ridgy billows, with a mighty cry,
Rush on the foamy beaches wild and bare;
No bark the madness of the waves will dare;
   The sailors sleep; the winds are loud and high;
   Ah, peerless Laura! for whose love I die,
Who gazes on thy smiles while I despair?
   As thus, in bitterness of heart, I cried,
I turned, and saw my Laura, kind and bright,
   A messenger of gladness, at my side:
To my poor bark she sprang with footstep light,
   And as we furrowed Tago's heaving tide,
I never saw so beautiful a night.

SONG.

FROM THE SPANISH OF IGLESIAS.

ALEXIS calls me cruel:
  The rifted crags that hold
The gathered ice of winter,
  He says, are not more cold.

When even the very blossoms
  Around the fountain's brim,
And forest walks, can witness
  The love I bear to him.

I would that I could utter
  My feelings without shame;
And tell him how I love him,
  Nor wrong my virgin fame.

Alas! to seize the moment
  When heart inclines to heart,
And press a suit with passion,
  Is not a woman's part.

If man come not to gather
  The roses where they stand,
They fade among their foliage;
  They cannot seek his hand.

THE COUNT OF GREIERS.

FROM THE GERMAN OF UHLAND.

AT morn the Count of Greiers before his castle stands;
He sees afar the glory that lights the mountain lands;
The horned crags are shining, and in the shade between
A pleasant Alpine valley lies beautifully green.

" Oh, greenest of the valleys, how shall I come to thee!
Thy herdsmen and thy maidens, how happy must
    they be!
I have gazed upon thee coldly, all lovely as thou art,
But the wish to walk thy pastures now stirs my in-
    most heart."

He hears a sound of timbrels, and suddenly appear
A troop of ruddy damsels and herdsmen drawing near;
They reach the castle greensward, and gayly dance
    across;
The white sleeves flit and glimmer, the wreaths and
    ribands toss.

The youngest of the maidens, slim as a spray of
    spring,
She takes the young count's fingers, and draws him to
    the ring,
They fling upon his forehead a crown of mountain
    flowers,
" And ho, young Count of Greiers! this morning thou
    art ours!"

Then hand in hand departing, with dance and roun-
    delay,
Through hamlet after hamlet, they lead the Count
    away.
They dance through wood and meadow, they dance
    across the linn,
Till the mighty Alpine summits have shut the music in.

The second morn is risen, and now the third is come;
Where stays the Count of Greiers? has he forgot his
    home?
Again the evening closes, in thick and sultry air;
There's thunder on the mountains, the storm is gath-
    ering there.

The cloud has shed its waters, the brook comes swol-
    len down;
You see it by the lightning—a river wide and brown.
Around a struggling swimmer the eddies dash and
    roar,
Till, seizing on a willow, he leaps upon the shore.

"Here am I cast by tempests far from your mountain
    dell.
Amid our evening dances the bursting deluge fell.
Ye all, in cots and caverns, have 'scaped the water-
    spout,
While me alone the tempest o'erwhelmed and hurried
    out.

"Farewell, with thy glad dwellers, green vale among
    the rocks!
Farewell the swift sweet moments, in which I watched
    thy flocks!
Why rocked they not my cradle in that delicious spot,
That garden of the happy, where Heaven endures
    me not?

"Rose of the Alpine valley! I feel, in every vein,
Thy soft touch on my fingers; oh, press them not
    again!
Bewitch me not, ye garlands, to tread that upward
    track,
And thou, my cheerless mansion, receive thy master
    back."

THE SERENADE.

FROM THE SPANISH.

If slumber, sweet Lisena!
   Have stolen o'er thine eyes,
As night steals o'er the glory
   Of spring's transparent skies;

Wake, in thy scorn and beauty,
   And listen to the strain
That murmurs my devotion,
   That mourns for thy disdain.

Here by thy door at midnight,
   I pass the dreary hour,
With plaintive sounds profaning
   The silence of thy bower;

A tale of sorrow cherished
   Too fondly to depart,
Of wrong from love the flatterer
   And my own wayward heart.

Twice, o'er this vale, the seasons
   Have brought and borne away
The January tempest, .
   The genial wind of May;

Yet still my plaint is uttered,
   My tears and sighs are given
To earth's unconscious waters,
   And wandering winds of heaven.

I saw, from this fair region,
   The smile of summer pass,
And myriad frost-stars glitter
   Among the russet grass.

While winter seized the streamlets
   That fled along the ground,
And fast in chains of crystal
   The truant murmurers bound.

I saw that to the forest
   The nightingales had flown,
And every sweet-voiced fountain
   Had hushed its silver tone.

The maniac winds, divorcing
   The turtle from his mate,
Raved through the leafy beeches,
   And left them desolate.

Now May, with life and music,
   The blooming valley fills,
And rears her flowery arches
   For all the little rills.

The minstrel bird of evening
   Comes back on joyous wings,
And, like the harp's soft murmur,
   Is heard the gush of springs.

And deep within the forest
  Are wedded turtles seen,
Their nuptial chambers seeking,
  Their chambers close and green.

The rugged trees are mingling
  Their flowery sprays in love;
The ivy climbs the laurel,
  To clasp the boughs above.

They change—but thou, Lisena,
  Art cold while I complain:
Why to thy lover only
  Should spring return in vain!

A NORTHERN LEGEND.

FROM THE GERMAN OF UHLAND.

THERE sits a lovely maiden,
  The ocean murmuring nigh;
She throws the hook, and watches;
  The fishes pass it by.

A ring, with a red jewel,
  Is sparkling on her hand;
Upon the hook she binds it,
  And flings it from the land.

Uprises from the water
  A hand like ivory fair.
What gleams upon its finger?
  The golden ring is there.

Uprises from the bottom
   A young and handsome knight;
In golden scales he rises,
   That glitter in the light.

The maid is pale with terror—
   "Nay, Knight of Ocean, nay,
It was not thou I wanted;
   Let go the ring, I pray."

"Ah, maiden, not to fishes
   The bait of gold is thrown;
The ring shall never leave me,
   And thou must be my own."

THE PARADISE OF TEARS.

FROM THE GERMAN OF N. MUELLER.

Beside the River of Tears, with branches low,
And bitter leaves, the weeping willows grow;
The branches stream like the dishevelled hair
Of women in the sadness of despair.

On rolls the stream with a perpetual sigh;
The rocks moan wildly as it passes by;
Hyssop and wormwood border all the strand,
And not a flower adorns the dreary land.

Then comes a child, whose face is like the sun,
And dips the gloomy waters as they run,
And waters all the region, and behold
The ground is bright with blossoms manifold.

Where fall the tears of love the rose appears,
And where the ground is bright with friendship's tears,
Forget-me-not, and violets, heavenly blue,
Spring, glittering with the cheerful drops like dew.

The souls of mourners, all whose tears are dried,
Like swans, come gently floating down the tide,
Walk up the golden sands by which it flows,
And in that Paradise of Tears repose.

There every heart rejoins its kindred heart;
There, in a long embrace that none may part,
Fulfilment meets desire, and that fair shore
Beholds its dwellers happy evermore.

THE LADY OF CASTLE WINDECK

FROM THE GERMAN OF CHAMISSO.

Rein in thy snorting charger!
  That stag but cheats thy sight;
He is luring thee on to Windeck,
  With his seeming fear and flight.

Now, where the mouldering turrets
  Of the outer gate arise,
The knight gazed over the ruins
  Where the stag was lost to his eyes.

The sun shone hot above him;
  The castle was still as death;
He wiped the sweat from his forehead,
  With a deep and weary breath.

"Who now will bring me a beaker
   Of the rich old wine that here,
In the choked-up vaults of Windeck,
   Has lain for many a year?"

The careless words had scarcely
   Time from his lips to fall,
When the Lady of Castle Windeck,
   Came round the ivy-wall.

He saw the glorious maiden
   In her snow-white drapery stand.
The bunch of keys at her girdle,
   The beaker high in her hand.

He quaffed that rich old vintage;
   With an eager lip he quaffed;
But he took into his bosom
   A fire with the grateful draught.

Her eyes' unfathomed brightness!
   The flowing gold of her hair!
He folded his hands in homage,
   And murmured a lover's prayer.

She gave him a look of pity,
   A gentle look of pain;
And quickly as he had seen her
   She passed from his sight again.

And ever, from that moment,
   He haunted the ruins there,
A sleepless, restless wanderer,
   A watcher with despair.

Ghost-like and pale he wandered,
  With a dreamy, haggard eye;
He seemed not one of the living,
  And yet he could not die.

'Tis said that the lady met him,
  When many years had past,
And kissing his lips, released him
  From the burden of life at last.

16

LATER POEMS.

TO THE APENNINES.

Your peaks are beautiful, ye Apennines!
  In the soft light of these serenest skies;
From the broad highland region, black with pines,
  Fair as the hills of Paradise they rise,
Bathed in the tint Peruvian slaves behold
In rosy flushes on the virgin gold.

There, rooted to the aërial shelves that wear
  The glory of a brighter world, might spring
Sweet flowers of heaven to scent the unbreathed air,
  And heaven's fleet messengers might rest the wing,
To view the fair earth in its summer sleep,
Silent, and cradled by the glimmering deep.

Below you lie men's sepulchres, the old
  Etrurian tombs, the graves of yesterday;
The herd's white bones lie mixed with human mould,
  Yet up the radiant steeps that I survey
Death never climbed, nor life's soft breath, with pain,
Was yielded to the elements again.

Ages of war have filled these plains with fear;
  How oft the hind has started at the clash
Of spears, and yell of meeting armies here,
  Or seen the lightning of the battle flash
From clouds, that rising with the thunder's sound,
Hung like an earth-born tempest o'er the ground!

Ah me! what armed nations—Asian horde,
  And Libyan host—the Scythian and the Gaul,
Have swept your base and through your passes poured,
  Like ocean-tides uprising at the call
Of tyrant winds—against your rocky side
The bloody billows dashed, and howled, and died.

How crashed the towers before beleaguering foes,
  Sacked cities smoked and realms were rent in twain;
And commonwealths against their rivals rose,
  Trode out their lives and earned the curse of Cain!
While, in the noiseless air and light that flowed
Round your fair brows, eternal Peace abode.

Here pealed the impious hymn, and altar-flames
  Rose to false gods, a dream-begotten throng,
Jove, Bacchus, Pan, and earlier, fouler names;
  While, as the unheeding ages passed along,
Ye, from your station in the middle skies,
Proclaimed the essential Goodness, strong and wise.

In you the heart that sighs for freedom seeks
  Her image; there the winds no barrier know,
Clouds come and rest and leave your fairy peaks;
  While even the immaterial Mind, below,
And Thought, her winged offspring, chained by power,
Pine silently for the redeeming hour.

EARTH. ·

A MIDNIGHT black with clouds is in the sky;
I seem to feel, upon my limbs, the weight
Of its vast brooding shadow.   All in vain
Turns the tired eye in search of form; no star
Pierces the pitchy veil; no ruddy blaze,
From dwellings lighted by the cheerful hearth,
Tinges the flowering summits of the grass.
No sound of life is heard, no village hum,
Nor measured tramp of footstep in the path,
Nor rush of wing, while, on the breast of Earth,
I lie and listen to her mighty voice:
A voice of many tones—sent up from streams
That wander through the gloom, from woods unseen,
Swayed by the sweeping of the tides of air,
From rocky chasms where darkness dwells all day,
And hollows of the great invisible hills,
And sands that edge the ocean, stretching far
Into the night—a melancholy sound!

O Earth! dost thou too sorrow for the past
Like man thy offspring?   Do I hear thee mourn
Thy childhood's unreturning hours, thy springs
Gone with their genial airs and melodies,
The gentle generations of thy flowers,
And thy majestic groves of olden time,
Perished with all their dwellers?   Dost thou wail
For that fair age of which the poets tell,
Ere yet the winds grew keen with frost, or fire
Fell with the rains, or spouted from the hills,
To blast thy greenness, while the virgin night
Was guiltless and salubrious as the day?
Or haply dost thou grieve for those that die—

For living things that trod thy paths awhile,
The love of thee and heaven—and now they sleep
Mixed with the shapeless dust on which thy herds
Trample and graze! I too must grieve with thee,
O'er loved ones lost. Their graves are far away
Upon thy mountains; yet, while I recline
Alone, in darkness, on thy naked soil,
The mighty nourisher and burial-place
Of man, I feel that I embrace their dust.

Ha! how the murmur deepens! I perceive
And tremble at its dreadful import. Earth
Uplifts a general cry for guilt and wrong,
And heaven is listening. The forgotten graves
Of the heart-broken utter forth their plaint.
The dust of her who loved and was betrayed,
And him who died neglected in his age;
The sepulchres of those who for mankind
Labored, and earned the recompense of scorn;
Ashes of martyrs for the truth, and bones
Of those who, in the strife for liberty,
Were beaten down, their corses given to dogs,
Their names to infamy, all find a voice.
The nook in which the captive, overtoiled,
Lay down to rest at last, and that which holds
Childhood's sweet blossoms, crushed by cruel hands,
Send up a plaintive sound. From battle-fields,
Where heroes madly drave and dashed their hosts
Against each other, rises up a noise,
As if the armed multitudes of dead
Stirred in their heavy slumber. Mournful tones
Come from the green abysses of the sea—
A story of the crimes the guilty sought
To hide beneath its waves. The glens, the groves,
Paths in the thicket, pools of running brook,
And banks and depths of lake, and streets and lanes
Of cities, now that living sounds are hushed,
Murmur of guilty force and treachery.

Here, where I rest, the vales of Italy
Are round me, populous from early time,   .
And field of the tremendous warfare waged
'Twixt good and evil.   Who, alas, shall dare
Interpret to man's ear the mingled voice
That comes from her old dungeons yawning now
To the black air, her amphitheatres,
Where the dew gathers on the mouldering stones,
And fanes of banished gods, and open tombs,
And roofless palaces, and streets and hearths
Of cities dug from their volcanic graves?
I hear a sound of many languages,
The utterance of nations now no more,
Driven out by mightier, as the days of heaven
Chase one another from the sky.   The blood
Of freemen shed by freemen, till strange lords
Came in their hour of weakness, and made fast
The yoke that yet is worn, cries out to Heaven.

What then shall cleanse thy bosom, gentle Earth,
From all its painful memories of guilt?
The whelming flood, or the renewing fire,
Or the slow change of time? that so, at last,
The horrid tale of perjury and strife,
Murder and spoil, which men call history,
May seem a fable, like the inventions told
By poets of the gods of Greece.   O thou,
Who sittest far beyond the Atlantic deep,
Among the sources of thy glorious streams,
My native Land of Groves! a newer page
In the great record of the world is thine ;
Shall it be fairer?   Fear, and friendly hope,
And envy, watch the issue, while the lines,
By which thou shalt be judged, are written down.

THE KNIGHT'S EPITAPH.

THIS is the church which Pisa, great and free,
Reared to St. Catharine. How the time-stained walls,
That earthquakes shook not from their poise, appear
To shiver in the deep and voluble tones
Rolled from the organ! Underneath my feet
There lies the lid of a sepulchral vault.
The image of an armed knight is graven
Upon it, clad in perfect panoply—
Cuishes, and greaves, and cuirass, with barred helm,
Gauntleted hand, and sword, and blazoned shield.
Around, in Gothic characters, worn dim
By feet of worshippers, are traced his name,
And birth, and death, and words of eulogy.
Why should I pore upon them? This old tomb,
This effigy, the strange disused form
Of this inscription, eloquently show
His history. Let me clothe in fitting words
The thoughts they breathe, and frame his epitaph.

"He whose forgotten dust for centuries
Has lain beneath this stone, was one in whom
Adventure, and endurance, and emprise
Exalted the mind's faculties and strung
The body's sinews. Brave he was in fight,
Courteous in banquet, scornful of repose,
And bountiful, and cruel, and devout,   ·
And quick to draw the sword in private feud.
He pushed his quarrels to the death, yet prayed
The saints as fervently on bended knees
As ever shaven cenobite. He loved
As fiercely as he fought. He would have borne

The maid that pleased him from her bower by night.
To his hill-castle, as the eagle bears
His victim from the fold, and rolled the rocks
On his pursuers.   He aspired to see
His native Pisa queen and arbitress
Of cities: earnestly for her he raised
His voice in council, and affronted death
In battle-field, and climbed the galley's deck,
And brought the captured flag of Genoa back,
Or piled upon the Arno's crowded quay
The glittering spoils of the tamed Saracen.
He was not born to brook the stranger's yoke,
But would have joined the exiles that withdrew
For ever, when the Florentine broke in
The gates of Pisa, and bore off the bolts
For trophies—but he died before that day.

"He lived, the impersonation of an age
That never shall return.   His soul of fire
Was kindled by the breath of the rude time
He lived in.   Now a gentler race succeeds,
Shuddering at blood; the effeminate cavalier,
Turning his eyes from the reproachful past,
And from the hopeless future, gives to ease,
And love, and music, his inglorious life."

THE HUNTER OF THE PRAIRIES.

Ay, this is freedom!—these pure skies
    Were never stained with village smoke:
The fragrant wind, that through them flies,
    Is breathed from wastes by plough unbroke.

Here, with my rifle and my steed,
  And her who left the world for me,
I plant me, where the red deer feed
  In the green desert—and am free.

For here the fair savannas know
  No barriers in the bloomy grass;
Wherever breeze of heaven may blow,
  Or beam of heaven may glance, I pass.
In pastures, measureless as air,
  The bison is my noble game;
The bounding elk, whose antlers tear
  The branches, falls before my aim.

Mine are the river-fowl that scream
  From the long stripe of waving sedge;
The bear that marks my weapon's gleam,
  Hides vainly in the forest's edge;
In vain the she-wolf stands at bay;
  The brinded catamount, that lies
High in the boughs to watch his prey,
  Even in the act of springing, dies.

With what free growth the elm and plane
  Fling their huge arms across my way,
Gray, old, and cumbered with a train
  Of vines, as huge, and old, and gray!
Free stray the lucid streams, and find
  No taint in these fresh lawns and shades;
Free spring the flowers that scent the wind
  Where never scythe has swept the glades.

Alone the Fire, when frost-winds sere
  The heavy herbage of the ground,
Gathers his annual harvest here,
  With roaring like the battle's sound,

And hurrying flames that sweep the plain,
　And smoke-streams gushing up the sky:
I meet the flames with flames again,
　And at my door they cower and die.

Here, from dim woods, the aged past
　Speaks solemnly; and I behold
The boundless future in the vast
　And lonely river, seaward rolled.
Who feeds its founts with rain and dew·
　Who moves, I ask, its gliding mass,
And trains the bordering vines, whose blue
　Bright clusters tempt me as I pass?

Broad are these streams—my steed obeys,
　Plunges, and bears me through the tide.
Wide are these woods—I thread the maze
　Of giant stems, nor ask a guide.
I hunt till day's last glimmer dies
　O'er woody vale and grassy height;
And kind the voice and glad the eyes
　That welcome my return at night.

———————•◆•———————

SEVENTY-SIX.

What heroes from the woodland sprung,
　When, through the fresh awakened land,
The thrilling cry of freedom rung,
And to the work of warfare strung
　The yeoman's iron hand!

Hills flung the cry to hills around,
 And ocean-mart replied to mart,
And streams, whose springs were yet unfound,
Pealed far away the startling sound
 Into the forest's heart.

Then marched the brave from rocky steep,
 From mountain river swift and cold;
The borders of the stormy deep,
The vales where gathered waters sleep,
 Sent up the strong and bold,—

As if the very earth again
 Grew quick with God's creating breath,
And, from the sods of grove and glen,
Rose ranks of lion-hearted men
 To battle to the death.

The wife, whose babe first smiled that day,
 The fair fond bride of yestereve,
And aged sire and matron gray,
Saw the loved warriors haste away,
 And deemed it sin to grieve.

Already had the strife begun;
 Already blood, on Concord's plain,
Along the springing grass had run,
And blood had flowed at Lexington,
 Like brooks of April rain.

That death-stain on the vernal sward
 Hallowed to freedom all the shore;
In fragments fell the yoke abhorred—
The footstep of a foreign lord
 Profaned the soil no more.

THE LIVING LOST.

MATRON! the children of whose love,
  Each to his grave, in youth have passed,
And now the mould is heaped above
  The dearest and the last!
Bride! who dost wear the widow's veil
Before the wedding flowers are pale!
Ye deem the human heart endures
No deeper, bitterer grief than yours.

Yet there are pangs of keener wo,
  Of which the sufferers never speak,
Nor to the world's cold pity show
  The tears that scald the cheek,
Wrung from their eyelids by the shame
And guilt of those they shrink to name,
Whom once they loved with cheerful will,
And love, though fallen and branded, still

Weep, ye who sorrow for the dead,
  Thus breaking hearts their pain relieve;
And reverenced are the tears ye shed,
  And honored ye who grieve.
The praise of those who sleep in earth,
The pleasant memory of their worth,
The hope to meet when life is past,
Shall heal the tortured mind at last.

But ye, who for the living lost
  That agony in secret bear,
Who shall with soothing words accost
  The strength of your despair?

Grief for your sake is scorn for them
Whom ye lament and all condemn;
And o'er the world of spirits lies
A gloom from which ye turn your eyes.

———•••———

CATTERSKILL FALLS.

MIDST greens and shades the Catterskill leaps,
   From cliffs where the wood-flower clings;
All summer he moistens his verdant steeps
   With the sweet light spray of the mountain springs;
And he shakes the woods on the mountain side,
When they drip with the rains of autumn-tide.

But when, in the forest bare and old,
   The blast of December calls,
He builds, in the starlight clear and cold,
   A palace of ice where his torrent falls,
With turret, and arch, and fretwork fair,
And pillars blue as the summer air.

For whom are those glorious chambers wrought,
   In the cold and cloudless night!
Is there neither spirit nor motion of thought
   In forms so lovely, and hues so bright!
Hear what the gray-haired woodmen tell
Of this wild stream and its rocky dell.

'Twas hither a youth of dreamy mood,
   A hundred winters ago,
Had wandered over the mighty wood,
   When the panther's track was fresh on the snow,
And keen were the winds that came to stir
The long dark boughs of the hemlock fir.

17

Too gentle of mien he seemed and fair,
  For a child of those rugged steeps;
His home lay low in the valley where
  The kingly Hudson rolls to the deeps;
But he wore the hunter's frock that day,
And a slender gun on his shoulder lay.

And here he paused, and against the trunk
  Of a tall gray linden leant,
When the broad clear orb of the sun had sunk
  From his path in the frosty firmament,
And over the round dark edge of the hill
A cold green light was quivering still.

And the crescent moon, high over the green,
  From a sky of crimson shone,
On that icy palace, whose towers were seen
  To sparkle as if with stars of their own;
While the water fell with a hollow sound,
'Twixt the glistening pillars ranged around.

Is that a being of life, that moves
  Where the crystal battlements rise?
A maiden watching the moon she loves,
  At the twilight hour, with pensive eyes?
Was that a garment which seemed to gleam
Betwixt the eye and the falling stream?

'Tis only the torrent tumbling o'er,
  In the midst of those glassy walls,
Gushing, and plunging, and beating the floor
  Of the rocky basin in which it falls.
'Tis only the torrent—but why that start?
Why gazes the youth with a throbbing heart?

He thinks no more of his home afar,
  Where his sire and sister wait.
He heeds no longer how star after star

Looks forth on the night as the hour grows late.
He heeds not the snow-wreaths, lifted and cast
From a thousand boughs, by the rising blast.

His thoughts are alone of those who dwell
  In the halls of frost and snow,
Who pass where the crystal domes upswell
  From the alabaster floors below,
Where the frost-trees shoot with leaf and spray,
And frost-gems scatter a silvery day.

" And oh that those glorious haunts were mine ! "
  He speaks, and throughout the glen
Thin shadows swim in the faint moonshine,
  And take a ghastly likeness of men,
As if the slain by the wintry storms
Came forth to the air in their earthly forms.

There pass the chasers of seal and whale,
  With their weapons quaint and grim,
And bands of warriors in glittering mail,
  And herdsmen and hunters huge of limb.
There are naked arms, with bow and spear,
And furry gauntlets the carbine rear.

There are mothers—and oh how sadly their eyes
  On their children's white brows rest !
There are youthful lovers—the maiden lies,
  In a seeming sleep, on the chosen breast ;
There are fair wan women with moonstruck air,
The snow-stars flecking their long loose hair.

They eye him not as they pass along,
  But his hair stands up with dread,
When he feels that he moves with that phantom throng,
  Till those icy turrets are over his head,
And the torrent's roar as they enter seems
Like a drowsy murmur heard in dreams.

The glittering threshold is scarcely passed,
   When there gathers and wraps him round
A thick white twilight, sullen and vast,
   In which there is neither form nor sound;
The phantoms, the glory, vanish all,
With the dying voice of the waterfall.

Slow passes the darkness of that trance,
   And the youth now faintly sees
Huge shadows and gushes of light that dance
   On a rugged ceiling of unhewn trees,
And walls where the skins of beasts are hung,
And rifles glitter on antlers strung.

On a couch of shaggy skins he lies;
   As he strives to raise his head,
Hard-featured woodmen, with kindly eyes,
   Come round him and smooth his furry bed,
And bid him rest, for the evening star
Is scarcely set and the day is far.

They had found at eve the dreaming one
   By the base of that icy steep,
When over his stiffening limbs begun
   The deadly slumber of frost to creep,
And they cherished the pale and breathless form,
Till the stagnant blood ran free and warm.

THE STRANGE LADY

THE summer morn is bright and fresh, the birds are
    darting by,
As if they loved to breast the breeze that sweeps the
    cool clear sky;
Young Albert, in the forest's edge, has heard a rust-
    ling sound,
An arrow slightly strikes his hand and falls upon the
    ground.

A dark-haired woman from the wood comes suddenly
    in sight;
Her merry eye is full and black, her cheek is brown
    and bright;
Her gown is of the mid-sea blue, her belt with beads
    is strung,
And yet she speaks in gentle tones, and in the Eng-
    lish tongue.

" It was an idle bolt I sent, against the villain crow;
Fair sir, I fear it harmed thy hand; beshrew my err-
    ing bow!"
" Ah! would that bolt had not been spent! then,
    lady, might I wear
A lasting token on my hand of one so passing fair!"

" Thou art a flatterer like the rest, but wouldst thou
    take with me
A day of hunting in the wilds, beneath the green-
    wood tree,
I know where most the pheasants feed, and where
    the red-deer herd,
And thou shouldst chase the nobler game, and I
    bring down the bird."

Now Albert in her quiver lays the arrow in its place,
And wonders as he gazes on the beauty of her face:
"Those hunting-grounds are far away, and, lady,
		'twere not meet
That night, amid the wilderness, should overtake thy
		feet."

"Heed not the night; a summer lodge amid the wild
		is mine,—		.
'Tis shadowed by the tulip-tree, 'tis mantled by the vine;
The wild plum sheds its yellow fruit from fragrant
		thickets nigh,
And flowery prairies from the door stretch till they
		meet the sky.

"There in the boughs that hide the roof the mock-
		bird sits and sings,
And there the hang-bird's brood within its little ham-
		mock swings;
A pebbly brook, where rustling winds among the
		hopples sweep,
Shall lull thee till the morning sun looks in upon thy
		sleep."

Away, into the forest depths by pleasant paths they go,
He with his rifle on his arm, the lady with her bow,
Where cornels arch their cool dark boughs o'er beds
		of winter-green,
And never at his father's door again was Albert seen.

That night upon the woods came down a furious hur-
		ricane,
With howl of winds and roar of streams, and beating
		of the rain;
The mighty thunder broke and drowned the noises in
		its crash;
The old trees seemed to fight like fiends beneath the
		lightning-flash.

Next day, within a mossy glen, 'mid mouldering trunks
    were found
The fragments of a human form upon the bloody
    ground;
White bones from which the flesh was torn, and locks
    of glossy hair;
They laid them in the place of graves, yet wist not
    whose they were.

And whether famished evening wolves had mangled
    Albert so,
Or that strange dame so gay and fair were some mys-
    terious foe,
Or whether to that forest lodge, beyond the moun-
    tains blue,
He went to dwell with her, the friends who mourned
    him never knew.

LIFE.

On Life! I breathe thee in the breeze,
    I feel thee bounding in my veins,
I see thee in these stretching trees,
    These flowers, this still rock's mossy stains.

This stream of odors flowing by
    From clover-field and clumps of pine,
This music, thrilling all the sky,
    From all the morning birds, are thine.

Thou fill'st with joy this little one,
    That leaps and shouts beside me here,
Where Isar's clay-white rivulets run
    Through the dark woods like frighted deer

Ah! must thy mighty breath, that wakes
    Insect and bird, and flower and tree,
From the low trodden dust, and makes
    Their daily gladness, pass from me—

Pass, pulse by pulse, till o'er the ground
    These limbs, now strong, shall creep with pain,
And this fair world of sight and sound
    Seem fading into night again?

The things, oh LIFE! thou quickenest, all
    Strive upward towards the broad bright sky,
Upward and outward, and they fall
    Back to earth's bosom when they die.

All that have borne the touch of death,
    All that shall live, lie mingled there,
Beneath that veil of bloom and breath,
    That living zone 'twixt earth and air.

There lies my chamber dark and still,
    The atoms trampled by my feet,
There wait, to take the place I fill
    In the sweet air and sunshine sweet.

Well, I have had my turn, have been
    Raised from the darkness of the clod,
And for a glorious moment seen
    The brightness of the skirts of God;

And knew the light within my breast,
    Though wavering oftentimes and dim,
The power, the will, that never rest,
    And cannot die, were all from him.

Dear child! I know that thou wilt grieve
  To see me taken from thy love,
Wilt seek my grave at Sabbath eve,
  And weep, and scatter flowers above.

Thy little heart will soon be healed,
  And being shall be bliss, till thou
To younger forms of life must yield
  The place thou fill'st with beauty now.

When we descend to dust again,
  Where will the final dwelling be
Of thought and all its memories then,
  My love for thee, and thine for me!

"EARTH'S CHILDREN CLEAVE TO EARTH."

EARTH's children cleave to Earth—her frail
  Decaying children dread decay.
You wreath of mist that leaves the vale,
  And lessens in the morning ray:
Look, how, by mountain rivulet,
  It lingers as it upward creeps,
And clings to fern and copsewood set
  Along the green and dewy steeps:
Clings to the flowery kalmia, clings
  To precipices fringed with grass,
Dark maples where the wood-thrush sings,
  And bowers of fragrant sassafras.
Yet all in vain—it passes still
  From hold to hold, it cannot stay,
And in the very beams that fill
  The world with glory, wastes away,

Till, parting from the mountain's brow,
    It vanishes from human eye,
And that which sprung of earth is now
    A portion of the glorious sky.

THE HUNTER'S VISION.

Upon a rock that, high and sheer,
    Rose from the mountain's breast.
A weary hunter of the deer
    Had sat him down to rest,
And bared to the soft summer air
His hot red brow and sweaty hair.

All dim in haze the mountains lay,
    With dimmer vales between;
And rivers glimmered on their way,
    By forests faintly seen;
While ever rose a murmuring sound,
From brooks below and bees around.

He listened, till he seemed to hear
    A strain, so soft and low,
That whether in the mind or ear
    The listener scarce might know.
With such a tone, so sweet, so mild,
The watching mother lulls her child.

"Thou weary huntsman," thus it said,
    "Thou faint with toil and heat,
The pleasant land of rest is spread
    Before thy very feet,
And those whom thou wouldst gladly see
Are waiting there to welcome thee."

He looked, and 'twixt the earth and sky
　Amid the noontide haze,
A shadowy region met his eye,
　And grew beneath his gaze,
As if the vapors of the air
Had gathered into shapes so fair.

Groves freshened as he looked, and flowers
　Showed bright on rocky bank,
And fountains welled beneath the bowers,
　Where deer and pheasant drank.
He saw the glittering streams, he heard
The rustling bough and twittering bird.

And friends, the dead, in boyhood dear
　There lived and walked again,
And there was one who many a year
　Within her grave had lain,
A fair young girl, the hamlet's pride—
His heart was breaking when she died:

Bounding, as was her wont, she came
　Right towards his resting-place,
And stretched her hand and called his name
　With that sweet smiling face.
Forward with fixed and eager eyes,
The hunter leaned in act to rise:

Forward he leaned, and headlong down
　Plunged from that craggy wall;
He saw the rocks, steep, stern, and brown,
　An instant, in his fall;
A frightful instant—and no more,
The dream and life at once were o'er.

THE GREEN MOUNTAIN BOYS.

I.

Here we halt our march, and pitch our tent
  On the rugged forest ground,
And light our fire with the branches rent
  By winds from the beeches round.
Wild storms have torn this ancient wood,
  But a wilder is at hand,
With hail of iron and rain of blood,
  To sweep and waste the land.

II.

How the dark wood rings with voices shrill,
  That startle the sleeping bird;
To-morrow eve must the voice be still,
  And the step must fall unheard.
The Briton lies by the blue Champlain,
  In Ticonderoga's towers,
And ere the sun rise twice again,
  Must they and the lake be ours.

III.

Fill up the bowl from the brook that glides
  Where the fire-flies light the brake;
A ruddier juice the Briton hides
  In his fortress by the lake.
Build high the fire, till the panther leap
  From his lofty perch in flight,
And we'll strengthen our weary arms with sleep
  For the deeds of to-morrow night.

A PRESENTIMENT.

"Oh father, let us hence—for hark,
  A fearful murmur shakes the air;
The clouds are coming swift and dark;—
  What horrid shapes they wear!
A winged giant sails the sky;
Oh father, father, let us fly!"

"Hush, child; it is a grateful sound,
  That beating of the summer shower;
Here, where the boughs hang close around,
  We'll pass a pleasant hour,
Till the fresh wind, that brings the rain,
Has swept the broad heaven clear again."

"Nay, father, let us haste—for see,
  That horrid thing with horned brow,—
His wings o'erhang this very tree,
  He scowls upon us now;
His huge black arm is lifted high;
Oh father, father, let us fly!"

"Hush, child;" but, as the father spoke,
  Downward the livid firebolt came,
Close to his ear the thunder broke,
  And, blasted by the flame,
The child lay dead; while dark and still,
Swept the grim cloud along the hill.

18

THE CHILD'S FUNERAL.

Fair is thy sight, Sorrento, green thy shore,
　Black crags behind thee pierce the clear blue skies;
The sea, whose borderers ruled the world of yore,
　As clear and bluer still before thee lies.

Vesuvius smokes in sight, whose fount of fire,
　Outgushing, drowned the cities on his steeps;
And murmuring Naples, spire o'ertopping spire,
　Sits on the slope beyond where Virgil sleeps.

Here doth the earth, with flowers of every hue,
　Heap her green breast when April suns are bright
Flowers of the morning-red, or ocean-blue,
　Or like the mountain frost of silvery white.

Currents of fragrance, from the orange tree,
　And sward of violets, breathing to and fro,
Mingle, and wandering out upon the sea,
　Refresh the idle boatsman where they blow.

Yet even here, as under harsher climes,
　Tears for the loved and early lost are shed;
That soft air saddens with the funeral chimes,
　Those shining flowers are gathered for the dead.

Here once a child, a smiling playful one,
　All the day long caressing and caressed,
Died when its little tongue had just begun
　To lisp the names of those it loved the best.

The father strove his struggling grief to quell,
  The mother wept as mothers use to weep,
Two little sisters wearied them to tell
  When their dear Carlo would awake from sleep.

Within an inner room his couch they spread,
  His funeral couch; with mingled grief and love,
They laid a crown of roses on his head,
  And murmured, "Brighter is his crown above."

They scattered round him, on the snowy sheet,
  Laburnum's strings of sunny-colored gems,
Sad hyacinths, and violets dim and sweet,
  And orange-blossoms on their dark green stems.

And now the hour is come, the priest is there;
  Torches are lit and bells are tolled; they go,
With solemn rites of blessing and of prayer,
  To lay the little one in earth below.

The door is opened; hark! that quick glad cry;
  Carlo has waked, has waked, and is at play;
The little sisters laugh and leap, and try
  To climb the bed on which the infant lay.

And there he sits alive, and gayly shakes
  In his full hands, the blossoms red and white,
And smiles with winking eyes, like one who wakes
  From long deep slumbers at the morning light.

THE BATTLE-FIELD.

Once this soft turf, this rivulet's sands,
  Were trampled by a hurrying crowd.
And fiery hearts and armed hands
  Encountered in the battle-cloud.

Ah! never shall the land forget
  How gushed the life-blood of her brave—
Gushed, warm with hope and courage yet,
  Upon the soil they fought to save.

Now all is calm, and fresh, and still,
  Alone the chirp of flitting bird,
And talk of children on the hill,
  And bell of wandering kine are heard.

No solemn host goes trailing by
  The black-mouthed gun and staggering wain;
Men start not at the battle-cry,
  Oh, be it never heard again!

Soon rested those who fought; but thou
  Who minglest in the harder strife
For truths which men receive not now,
  Thy warfare only ends with life.

A friendless warfare! lingering long
  Through weary day and weary year.
A wild and many-weaponed throng
  Hang on thy front, and flank, and rear.

Yet nerve thy spirit to the proof,
  And blench not at thy chosen lot.
The timid good may stand aloof,
  The sage may frown—yet faint thou not.

Nor heed the shaft too surely cast,
  The foul and hissing bolt of scorn;
For with thy side shall dwell, at last,
  The victory of endurance born.

Truth, crushed to earth, shall rise again;
  The eternal years of God are hers;
But Error, wounded, writhes in pain,
  And dies among his worshippers.

Yea, though thou lie upon the dust,
  When they who helped thee flee in fear,
Die full of hope and manly trust,
  Like those who fell in battle here.

Another hand thy sword shall wield,
  Another hand the standard wave,
Till from the trumpet's mouth is pealed
  The blast of triumph o'er thy grave.

THE·FUTURE LIFE.

How shall I know thee in the sphere which keeps
  The disembodied spirits of the dead,
When all of thee that time could wither sleeps
  And perishes among the dust we tread!

For I shall feel the sting of ceaseless pain
    If there I meet thy gentle presence not;
Nor hear the voice I love, nor read again
    In thy serenest eyes the tender thought.

Will not thy own meek heart demand me there!
    That heart whose fondest throbs to me were given
My name on earth was ever in thy prayer,
    And wilt thou never utter it in heaven!

In meadows fanned by heaven's life-breathing wind,
    In the resplendence of that glorious sphere,
And larger movements of the unfettered mind,
    Wilt thou forget the love that joined us here?

The love that lived through all the stormy past,
    And meekly with my harsher nature bore,
And deeper grew, and tenderer to the last,
    Shall it expire with life, and be no more?

A happier lot than mine, and larger light,
    Await thee there; for thou hast bowed thy will
In cheerful homage to the rule of right,
    And lovest all, and renderest good for ill.

For me, the sordid cares in which I dwell,
    Shrink and consume my heart, as heat the scroll;
And wrath has left its scar—that fire of hell
    Has left its frightful scar upon my soul.

Yet though thou wear'st the glory of the sky,
    Wilt thou not keep the same beloved name,
The same fair thoughtful brow, and gentle eye,
    Lovelier in heaven's sweet climate, yet the same!

Shalt thou not teach me, in that calmer home,
    The wisdom that I learned so ill in this—
The wisdom which is love—till I become
    Thy fit companion in that land of bliss!

THE DEATH OF SCHILLER.

'Tis said, when Schiller's death drew nigh,
  The wish possessed his mighty mind,
To wander forth wherever lie
  The homes and haunts of human-kind.

Then strayed the poet, in his dreams,
  By Rome and Egypt's ancient graves;
Went up the New World's forest streams,
  Stood in the Hindoo's temple-caves;

Walked with the Pawnee, fierce and stark,
  The sallow Tartar, midst his herds,
The peering Chinese, and the dark
  False Malay uttering gentle words.

How could he rest? even then he trod
  The threshold of the world unknown;
Already, from the seat of God,
  A ray upon his garments shone;—

Shone and awoke the strong desire
  For love and knowledge reached not here,
Till, freed by death, his soul of fire
  Sprang to a fairer, ampler sphere.

THE FOUNTAIN.

Fountain, that springest on this grassy slope,
Thy quick cool murmur mingles pleasantly,
With the cool sound of breezes in the beech,
Above me in the noontide. Thou dost wear
No stain of thy dark birthplace; gushing up
From the red mould and slimy roots of earth,
Thou flashest in the sun. The mountain air,
In winter, is not clearer, nor the dew
That shines on mountain blossom. Thus doth God
Bring, from the dark and foul, the pure and bright.

This tangled thicket on the bank above
Thy basin, how thy waters keep it green!
For thou dost feed the roots of the wild vine
That trails all over it, and to the twigs
Ties fast her clusters. There the spice-bush lifts
Her leafy lances; the viburnum there,
Paler of foliage, to the sun holds up
Her circlet of green berries. In and out
The chipping sparrow, in her coat of brown,
Steals silently, lest I should mark her nest.

Not such thou wert of yore, ere yet the axe
Had smitten the old woods. Then hoary trunks
Of oak, and plane, and hickory, o'er thee held
A mighty canopy. When April winds
Grew soft, the maple burst into a flush
Of scarlet flowers. The tulip-tree, high up,
Opened, in airs of June, her multitude
Of golden chalices to humming-birds
And silken-winged insects of the sky.

Frail wood-plants clustered round thy edge in Spring.
The liverleaf put forth her sister blooms
Of faintest blue.   Here the quick-footed wolf,
Passing to lap thy waters, crushed the flower
Of sanguinaria, from whose brittle stem
The red drops fell like blood.   The deer, too, left
Her delicate foot-print in the soft moist mould,
And on the fallen leaves.   The slow-paced bear,
In such a sultry summer noon as this,
Stopped at thy stream, and drank, and leaped across.

But thou hast histories that stir the heart
With deeper feeling; while I look on thee
They rise before me.   I behold the scene
Hoary again with forests; I behold
The Indian warrior, whom a hand unseen
Has smitten with his death-wound in the woods,
Creep slowly to thy well-known rivulet,
And slake his death-thirst.   Hark, that quick fierce cry
That rends the utter silence; 'tis the whoop
Of battle, and a throng of savage men
With naked arms and faces stained like blood,
Fill the green wilderness; the long bare arms
Are heaved aloft, bows twang and arrows stream ;
Each makes a tree his shield, and every tree
Sends forth its arrow.   Fierce the fight and short,
As is the whirlwind.   Soon the conquerors
And conquered vanish, and the dead remain
Mangled by tomahawks.   The mighty woods
Are still again, the frighted bird comes back
And plumes her wings; but thy sweet waters run
Crimson with blood.   Then, as the sun goes down,
Amid the deepening twilight I descry
Figures of men that crouch and creep unheard,
And bear away the dead.   The next day's shower
Shall wash the tokens of the fight away.

I look again—a hunter's lodge is built,
With poles and boughs, beside thy crystal well,
While the meek autumn stains the woods with gold,
And sheds his golden sunshine.   To the door
The red man slowly drags the enormous bear
Slain in the chestnut thicket, or flings down
The deer from his strong shoulders.   Shaggy fells
Of wolf and cougar hang upon the walls,
And loud the black-eyed Indian maidens laugh,
That gather, from the rustling heaps of leaves,
The hickory's white nuts, and the dark fruit
That falls from the gray butternut's long boughs.

So centuries passed by, and still the woods
Blossomed in spring, and reddened when the year
Grew chill, and glistened in the frozen rains
Of winter, till the white man swung the axe
Beside thee—signal of a mighty change.
Then all around was heard the crash of trees,
Trembling awhile and rushing to the ground,
The low of ox, and shouts of men who fired
The brushwood, or who tore the earth with ploughs
The grain sprang thick and tall, and hid in green
The blackened hill-side; ranks of spiky maize
Rose like a host embattled; the buckwheat
Whitened broad acres, sweetening with its flowers
The August wind.   White cottages were seen
With rose-trees at the windows; barns from which
Came loud and shrill the crowing of the cock;
Pastures where rolled and neighed the lordly horse,
And white flocks browsed and bleated.   A rich turf
Of grasses brought from far o'ercrept thy bank,   ˙
Spotted with the white clover.   Blue-eyed girls
Brought pails, and dipped them in thy crystal pool;
And children, ruddy-cheeked and flaxen-haired,
Gathered the glistening cowslip from thy edge.

Since then, what steps have trod thy border!   Here
On thy green bank, the woodman of the swamp

Has laid his axe, the reaper of the hill
His sickle, as they stooped to taste thy stream.
The sportsman, tired with wandering in the still
September noon, has bathed his heated brow
In thy cool current.   Shonting boys, let loose
For a wild holiday, have quaintly shaped
Into a cup the folded linden leaf,
And dipped thy sliding crystal.   From the wars
Returning, the plumed soldier by thy side
Has sat, and mused how pleasant 'twere to dwell
In such a spot, and be as free as thou,
And move for no man's bidding more.   At eve,
When thou wert crimson with the crimson sky,
Lovers have gazed upon thee, and have thought
Their mingled lives should flow as peacefully
And brightly as thy waters.   Here the sage,
Gazing into thy self-replenished depth,
Has seen eternal order circumscribe
And bind the motions of eternal change,
And from the gushing of thy simple fount
Has reasoned to the mighty universe.

   Is there no other change for thee, that lurks
Among the future ages!   Will not man
Seek out strange arts to wither and deform
The pleasant landscape which thou makest green!
Or shall the veins that feed thy constant stream
Be choked in middle earth, and flow no more
For ever, that the water-plants along
Thy channel perish, and the bird in vain
Alight to drink!   Haply shall these green hills
Sink, with the lapse of years, into the gulf
Of ocean waters, and thy source be lost
Amidst the bitter brine!   Or shall they rise,
Upheaved in broken cliffs and airy peaks,
Haunts of the eagle and the snake, and thou
Gush midway from the bare and barren steep!

THE WINDS.

I.

YE winds, ye unseen currents of the air,
 Softly ye played a few brief hours ago;
Ye bore the murmuring bee; ye tossed the hair
O'er maiden cheeks, that took a fresher glow:
Ye rolled the round white cloud through depths of blue;
Ye shook from shaded flowers the lingering dew;
Before you the catalpa's blossoms flew,
 Light blossoms, dropping on the grass like snow.

II.

How are ye changed! Ye take the cataract's sound;
 Ye take the whirlpool's fury and its might;
The mountain shudders as ye sweep the ground;
 The valley woods lie prone beneath your flight.
The clouds before you shoot like eagles past;
The homes of men are rocking in your blast;
Ye lift the roofs like autumn leaves, and cast,
 Skyward, the whirling fragments out of sight.

III.

The weary fowls of heaven make wing in vain,
 To escape your wrath; ye seize and dash them dead;
Against the earth ye drive the roaring rain;
 The harvest-field becomes a river's bed;
And torrents tumble from the hills around,
Plains turn to lakes, and villages are drowned,
And wailing voices, midst the tempest's sound,
 Rise, as the rushing waters swell and spread.

IV.

Ye dart upon the deep, and straight is heard
  A wilder roar, and men grow pale, and pray;
Ye fling its floods around you, as a bird
  Flings o'er his shivering plumes the fountain's spray.
See! to the breaking mast the sailor clings;
Ye scoop the ocean to its briny springs,
And take the mountain billow on your wings,
  And pile the wreck of navies round the bay.

V.

Why rage ye thus?—no strife for liberty
  Has made you mad; no tyrant, strong through fear,
Has chained your pinions till ye wrenched them free,
  And rushed into the unmeasured atmosphere;
For ye were born in freedom where ye blow;
Free o'er the mighty deep to come and go;
Earth's solemn woods were yours, her wastes of snow,
  Her isles where summer blossoms all the year.

VI.

O ye wild winds! a mightier Power than yours
  In chains upon the shore of Europe lies;
The sceptred throng, whose fetters he endures,
  Watch his mute throes with terror in their eyes:
And armed warriors all around him stand,
And, as he struggles, tighten every band,
And lift the heavy spear, with threatening hand,
  To pierce the victim, should he strive to rise.

VII.

Yet oh, when that wronged Spirit of our race
  Shall break, as soon he must, his long-worn chains,
And leap in freedom from his prison-place,
  Lord of his ancient hills and fruitful plains,
19

Let him not rise, like these mad winds of air,
To waste the loveliness that time could spare,
To fill the earth with wo, and blot her fair
    Unconscious breast with blood from human veins.

VIII.

But may he like the spring-time come abroad,
    Who crumbles winter's gyves with gentle might,
When in the genial breeze, the breath of God,
    Come spouting up the unsealed springs to light;
Flowers start from their dark prisons at his feet,
The woods, long dumb, awake to hymnings sweet,
And morn and eve, whose glimmerings almost meet,
    Crowd back to narrow bounds the ancient night.

THE OLD MAN'S COUNSEL.

AMONG our hills and valleys, I have known
Wise and grave men, who, while their diligent hands
Tended or gathered in the fruits of earth,
Were reverent learners in the solemn school
Of nature.   Not in vain to them were sent
Seed-time and harvest, or the vernal shower
That darkened the brown tilth, or snow that beat
On the white winter hills.   Each brought, in turn,
Some truth, some lesson on the life of man,
Or recognition of the Eternal mind
Who veils his glory with the elements.

One such I knew long since, a white-haired man,
Pithy of speech, and merry when he would;
A genial optimist, who daily drew
From what he saw his quaint moralities.

Kindly he held communion, though so old,
With me a dreaming boy, and taught me much
That books tell not, and I shall ne'er forget.

The sun of May was bright in middle heaven,
And steeped the sprouting forests, the green hills
And emerald wheat-fields, in his yellow light.
Upon the apple-tree, where rosy buds
Stood clustered, ready to burst forth in bloom,
The robin warbled forth his full clear note
For hours, and wearied not. Within the woods,
Whose young and half transparent leaves scarce cast
A shade, gay circles of anemones
Danced on their stalks; the shadbush, white with
   flowers,
Brightened the glens; the new-leaved butternut
And quivering poplar to the roving breeze
Gave a balsamic fragrance. In the fields
I saw the pulses of the gentle wind
On the young grass. My heart was touched with joy
At so much beauty, flushing every hour
Into a fuller beauty; but my friend,
The thoughtful ancient, standing at my side,
Gazed on it mildly sad. I asked him why.

"Well mayst thou join in gladness," he replied,
"With the glad earth, her springing plants and flowers,
And this soft wind, the herald of the green
Luxuriant summer. Thou art young like them,
And well mayst thou rejoice. But while the flight
Of seasons fills and knits thy spreading frame,
It withers mine, and thins my hair, and dims
These eyes, whose fading light shall soon be quenched
In utter darkness. Hearest thou that bird?"

I listened, and from midst the depth of woods
Heard the love-signal of the grouse, that wears
A sable ruff around his mottled neck;

Partridge they call him by our northern streams,
And pheasant by the Delaware.   He beat
'Gainst his barred sides his speckled wings, and made
A sound like distant thunder; slow the strokes
At first, then fast and faster, till at length
They passed into a murmur and were still.

  "There hast thou," said my friend, "a fitting type
Of human life.   'Tis an old truth, I know,
But images like these revive the power
Of long familiar truths.   Slow pass our days
In childhood, and the hours of light are long
Betwixt the morn and eve; with swifter lapse
They glide in manhood, and in age they fly;
Till days and seasons flit before the mind
As flit the snow-flakes in a winter storm,
Seen rather than distinguished.   Ah! I seem
As if I sat within a helpless bark,
By swiftly running waters hurried on
To shoot some mighty cliff.   Along the banks
Grove after grove, rock after frowning rock,
Bare sands and pleasant homes, and flowery nooks,
And isles and whirlpools in the stream, appear
Each after each, but the devoted skiff
Darts by so swiftly that their images
Dwell not upon the mind, or only dwell
In dim confusion; faster yet I sweep
By other banks, and the great gulf is near.

  "Wisely, my son, while yet thy days are long,
And this fair change of seasons passes slow,
Gather and treasure up the good they yield—
All that they teach of virtue, of pure thoughts
And kind affections, reverence for thy God
And for thy brethren; so when thou shalt come
Into these barren years, thou mayst not bring
A mind unfurnished and a withered heart."

Long since that white-haired ancient slept—but still,
When the red flower-buds crowd the orchard bough,
And the ruffed grouse is drumming far within
The woods, his venerable form again
Is at my side, his voice is in my ear.

————•••————

IN MEMORY OF WILLIAM LEGGETT.

THE earth may ring from shore to shore,
　　With echoes of a glorious name,
But he, whose loss our tears deplore,
　　Has left behind him more than fame.

For when the death-frost came to lie
　　On Leggett's warm and mighty heart,
And quenched his bold and friendly eye,
　　His spirit did not all depart.

The words of fire that from his pen
　　Were flung upon the fervent page,
Still move, still shake the hearts of men,
　　Amid a cold and coward age.

His love of truth, too warm, too strong
　　For Hope or Fear to chain or chill,
His hate of tyranny and wrong,
　　Burn in the breasts he kindled still.

AN EVENING REVERY.

THE summer day is closed—the sun is set:
Well they have done their office, those bright hours,
The latest of whose train goes softly out
In the red West. The green blade of the ground
Has risen, and herds have cropped it; the young twig
Has spread its plaited tissues to the sun;
Flowers of the garden and the waste have blown
And withered; seeds have fallen upon the soil,
From bursting cells, and in their graves await
Their resurrection. Insects from the pools
Have filled the air awhile with humming wings,
That now are still for ever; painted moths
Have wandered the blue sky, and died again;
The mother-bird hath broken for her brood
Their prison shell, or shoved them from the nest,
Plumed for their earliest flight. In bright alcoves,
In woodland cottages with barky walls,
In noisome cells of the tumultuous town,
Mothers have clasped with joy the new-born babe.
Graves by the lonely forest, by the shore
Of rivers and of ocean, by the ways
Of the thronged city, have been hollowed out
And filled, and closed. This day hath parted friends
That ne'er before were parted; it hath knit
New friendships; it hath seen the maiden plight
Her faith, and trust her peace to him who long
Had wooed; and it hath heard, from lips which late
Were eloquent with love, the first harsh word,
That told the wedded one her peace was flown.
Farewell to the sweet sunshine! One glad day
Is added now to Childhood's merry days,
And one calm day to those of quiet Age.

Still the fleet hours run on; and as I lean,
Amid the thickening darkness, lamps are lit,
By those who watch the dead, and those who twine
Flowers for the bride. The mother from the eyes
Of her sick infant shades the painful light,
And sadly listens to his quick-drawn breath.

Oh thou great Movement of the Universe,
Or Change, or Flight of Time—for ye are one!
That bearest, silently, this visible scene
Into night's shadow and the streaming rays
Of starlight, whither art thou bearing me?
I feel the mighty current sweep me on,
Yet know not whither. Man foretells afar
The courses of the stars; the very hour
He knows when they shall darken or grow bright;
Yet doth the eclipse of Sorrow and of Death
Come unforewarned. Who next, of those I love,
Shall pass from life, or, sadder yet, shall fall
From virtue? Strife with foes, or bitterer strife
With friends, or shame and general scorn of men—
Which who can bear?—or the fierce rack of pain,
Lie they within my path? Or shall the years
Push me, with soft and inoffensive pace,
Into the stilly twilight of my age?
Or do the portals of another life
Even now, while I am glorying in my strength,
Impend around me? Oh! beyond that bourne,
In the vast cycle of being which begins
At that broad threshold, with what fairer forms
Shall the great law of change and progress clothe
Its workings? Gently—so have good men taught—
Gently, and without grief, the old shall glide
Into the new; the eternal flow of things,
Like a bright river of the fields of heaven,
Shall journey onward in perpetual peace.

THE PAINTED CUP.

THE fresh savannas of the Sangamon
Here rise in gentle swells, and the long grass
Is mixed with rustling hazels. Scarlet tufts
Are glowing in the green, like flakes of fire,
The wanderers of the prairie know them well,
And call that brilliant flower the Painted Cup.

Now, if thou art a poet, tell me not
That these bright chalices were tinted thus
To hold the dew for fairies, when they meet
On moonlight evenings in the hazel bowers,
And dance till they are thirsty. Call not up,
Amid this fresh and virgin solitude,
The faded fancies of an elder world;
But leave these scarlet cups to spotted moths
Of June, and glistening flies, and humming-birds,
To drink from, when on all these boundless lawns
The morning sun looks hot. Or let the wind
O'erturn in sport their ruddy brims, and pour
A sudden shower upon the strawberry plant,
To swell the reddening fruit that even now
Breathes a slight fragrance from the sunny slope.

But thou art of a gayer fancy. Well—
Let then the gentle Manitou of flowers,
Lingering amid the bloomy waste he loves,
Though all his swarthy worshippers are gone—
Slender and small, his rounded cheek all brown
And ruddy with the sunshine; let him come
On summer mornings, when the blossoms wake,
And part with little hands the spiky grass;
And touching, with his cherry lips, the edge
Of these bright beakers, drain the gathered dew.

A DREAM.

I HAD a dream—a strange, wild dream—
　Said a dear voice at early light;
And even yet its shadows seem
　To linger in my waking sight.

Earth, green with spring, and fresh with dew
　And bright with morn, before me stood;
And airs just wakened softly blew
　On the young blossoms of the wood.

Birds sang within the sprouting shade,
　Bees hummed amid the whispering grass,
And children prattled as they played
　Beside the rivulet's dimpling glass.

Fast climbed the sun: the flowers were flown,
　There played no children in the glen;
For some were gone, and some were grown
　To blooming dames and bearded men.

'Twas noon, 'twas summer: I beheld
　Woods darkening in the flush of day,
And that bright rivulet spread and swelled,
　A mighty stream, with creek and bay.

And here was love, and there was strife,
　And mirthful shouts, and wrathful cries,
And strong men, struggling as for life,
　With knotted limbs and angry eyes.

Now stooped the sun—the shades grew thin;
  The rustling paths were piled with leaves;
And sunburnt groups were gathering in,
  From the shorn field, its fruits and sheaves.

The river heaved with sullen sounds;
  The chilly wind was sad with moans;
Black hearses passed, and burial-grounds
  Grew thick with monumental stones.

Still waned the day; the wind that chased
  The jagged clouds blew chiller yet;
The woods were stripped, the fields were waste;
  The wintry sun was near his set.

And of the young, and strong, and fair,
  A lonely remnant, gray and weak,
Lingered, and shivered to the air
  Of that bleak shore and water bleak.

Ah! age is drear, and death is cold!
  I turned to thee, for thou wert near,
And saw thee withered, bowed, and old,
  And woke all faint with sudden fear.

'Twas thus I heard the dreamer say,
  And bade her clear her clouded brow;
"For thou and I, since childhood's day,
  Have walked in such a dream till now.

"Watch we in calmness, as they rise,
  The changes of that rapid dream,
And note its lessons, till our eyes
  Shall open in the morning beam."

THE ANTIQUITY OF FREEDOM.

HERE are old trees, tall oaks and gnarled pines,
That stream with gray-green mosses; here the ground
Was never trenched by spade, and flowers spring up
Unsown, and die ungathered. It is sweet
To linger here, among the flitting birds
And leaping squirrels, wandering brooks, and winds
That shake the leaves, and scatter, as they pass,
A fragrance from the cedars, thickly set
With pale blue berries. In these peaceful shades—
Peaceful, unpruned, immeasurably old—
My thoughts go up the long dim path of years,
Back to the earliest days of liberty.

Oh FREEDOM! thou art not, as poets dream,
A fair young girl, with light and delicate limbs,
And wavy tresses gushing from the cap
With which the Roman master crowned his slave
When he took off the gyves. A bearded man,
Armed to the teeth, art thou; one mailed hand
Grasps the broad shield, and one the sword; thy brow,
Glorious in beauty though it be, is scarred
With tokens of old wars; thy massive limbs
Are strong with struggling. Power at thee has launched
His bolts, and with his lightnings smitten thee;
They could not quench the life thou hast from heaven.
Merciless power has dug thy dungeon deep,
And his swart armorers, by a thousand fires,
Have forged thy chain; yet, while he deems thee bound,
The links are shivered, and the prison walls
Fall outward; terribly thou springest forth,

As springs the flame above a burning pile,
And shoutest to the nations, who return
Thy shoutings, while the pale oppressor flies.

Thy birthright was not given by human hands:
'Thou wert twin-born with man.   In pleasant fields,
While yet our race was few, thou sat'st with him,
To tend the quiet flock and watch the stars,
And teach the reed to utter simple airs.
Thou by his side, amid the tangled wood,
Didst war upon the panther and the wolf,
His only foes; and thou with him didst draw
The earliest furrow on the mountain side,
Soft with the deluge.   Tyranny himself,
Thy enemy, although of reverend look,
Hoary with many years, and far obeyed,
Is later born than thou; and as he meets
The grave defiance of thine elder eye
The usurper trembles in his fastnesses.

Thou shalt wax stronger with the lapse of years,
But he shall fade into a feebler age;
Feebler, yet subtler.   He shall weave his snares,
And spring them on thy careless steps, and clap
His withered hands, and from their ambush call
His hordes to fall upon thee.   He shall send
Quaint maskers, wearing fair and gallant forms
To catch thy gaze, and uttering graceful words
To charm thy ear; while his sly imps, by stealth,
Twine round thee threads of steel, light thread on thread
That grow to fetters; or bind down thy arms
With chains concealed in chaplets.   Oh! not yet
Mayst thou unbrace thy corslet, nor lay by
Thy sword; nor yet, O Freedom! close thy lids
In slumber; for thine enemy never sleeps,
And thou must watch and combat till the day
Of the new earth and heaven.   But wouldst thou rest
Awhile from tumult and the frauds of men,

These old and friendly solitudes invite
Thy visit. They, while yet the forest trees
Were young upon the unviolated earth,
And yet the moss-stains on the rock were new,
Beheld thy glorious childhood, and rejoiced.

----•••----

THE MAIDEN'S SORROW.

Seven long years has the desert rain
    Dropped on the clods that hide thy face;
Seven long years of sorrow and pain
    I have thought of thy burial-place.

Thought of thy fate in the distant west,
    Dying with none that loved thee near;
They who flung the earth on thy breast
    Turned from the spot without a tear.

There, I think, on that lonely grave,
    Violets spring in the soft May shower;
There, in the summer breezes, wave
    Crimson phlox and moccasin flower.

There the turtles alight, and there
    Feeds with her fawn the timid doe;
There, when the winter woods are bare,
    Walks the wolf on the crackling snow

Soon wilt thou wipe my tears away;
    All my task upon earth is done;
My poor father, old and gray,
    Slumbers beneath the churchyard stone.
20

In the dreams of my lonely bed,
   Ever thy form before me seems;
All night long I talk with the dead,
   All day long I think of my dreams.

This deep wound that bleeds and aches,
   This long pain, a sleepless pain—
When the Father my spirit takes,
   I shall feel it no more again.

THE RETURN OF YOUTH.

My friend, thou sorrowest for thy golden prime,
   For thy fair youthful years too swift of flight;
Thou musest, with wet eyes, upon the time
   Of cheerful hopes that filled the world with light,—
Years when thy heart was bold, thy hand was strong,
   And quick the thought that moved thy tongue to
      speak,
And willing faith was thine, and scorn of wrong
   Summoned the sudden crimson to thy cheek.

Thou lookest forward on the coming days,
   Shuddering to feel their shadow o'er thee creep;
A path, thick-set with changes and decays,
   Slopes downward to the place of common sleep;
And they who walked with thee in life's first stage,
   Leave one by one thy side, and, waiting near,
Thou seest the sad companions of thy age—
   Dull love of rest, and weariness and fear.

Yet grieve thou not, nor think thy youth is gone,
  Nor deem that glorious season e'er could die.
Thy pleasant youth, a little while withdrawn,
  Waits on the horizon of a brighter sky;
Waits, like the morn, that folds her wing and hides,
  Till the slow stars bring back her dawning hour;
. Waits, like the vanished spring, that slumbering bides
  Her own sweet time to waken bud and flower.

There shall he welcome thee, when thou shalt stand
  On his bright morning hills, with smiles more sweet
Than when at first he took thee by the hand,
  Through the fair earth to lead thy tender feet.
He shall bring back, but brighter, broader still,
  Life's early glory to thine eyes again,
Shall clothe thy spirit with new strength, and fill
  Thy leaping heart with warmer love than then.

. Hast thou not glimpses, in the twilight here,
  Of mountains where immortal morn prevails?
Comes there not, through the silence, to thine ear
  A gentle rustling of the morning gales;
A murmur, wafted from that glorious shore,
  Of streams that water banks for ever fair,
And voices of the loved ones gone before,
  More musical in that celestial air!

A HYMN OF THE SEA.

The sea is mighty, but a mightier sways
His restless billows. Thou, whose hands have scooped
His boundless gulfs and built his shore, thy breath,
That moved in the beginning o'er his face,

Moves o'er it evermore. The obedient waves
To its strong motion roll, and rise and fall.
Still from that realm of rain thy cloud goes up,
As at the first, to water the great earth,
And keep her valleys green. A hundred realms
Watch its broad shadow warping on the wind,
And in the dropping shower, with gladness hear
Thy promise of the harvest. I look forth
Over the boundless blue, where joyously
The bright crests of innumerable waves
Glance to the sun at once, as when the hands
Of a great multitude are upward flung
In acclamation. I behold the ships
Gliding from cape to cape, from isle to isle,
Or stemming toward far lands, or hastening home
From the old world. It is thy friendly breeze
That bears them, with the riches of the land,
And treasure of dear lives, till, in the port,
The shouting seaman climbs and furls the sail.

But who shall bide thy tempest, who shall face
The blast that wakes the fury of the sea?
Oh God! thy justice makes the world turn pale,
When on the armed fleet, that royally
Bears down the surges, carrying war, to smite
Some city, or invade some thoughtless realm,
Descends the fierce tornado. The vast hulks
Are whirled like chaff upon the waves; the sails
Fly, rent like webs of gossamer; the masts
Are snapped asunder; downward from the decks
Downward are slung, into the fathomless gulf,
Their cruel engines; and their hosts, arrayed
In trappings of the battle-field, are whelmed
By whirlpools, or dashed dead upon the rocks.
Then stand the nations still with awe, and pause,
A moment, from the bloody work of war.

These restless surges eat away the shores
Of earth's old continents; the fertile plain
Welters in shallows, headlands crumble down,
And the tide drifts the sea-sand in the streets
Of the drowned city. Thou, meanwhile, afar
In the green chambers of the middle sea,
Where broadest spread the waters and the line
Sinks deepest, while no eye beholds thy work,
Creator! thou dost teach the coral worm
To lay his mighty reefs. From age to age,
He builds beneath the waters, till, at last,
His bulwarks overtop the brine, and check
The long wave rolling from the southern pole
To break upon Japan. Thou bidd'st the fires,
That smoulder under ocean, heave on high
The new-made mountains, and uplift their peaks,
A place of refuge for the storm-driven bird.
The birds and wafting billows plant the rifts
With herb and tree; sweet fountains gush; sweet airs
Ripple the living lakes that, fringed with flowers,
Are gathered in the hollows. Thou dost look
On thy creation and pronounce it good.
Its valleys, glorious with their summer green,
Praise thee in silent beauty, and its woods,
Swept by the murmuring winds of ocean, join
The murmuring shores in a perpetual hymn.

NOON.

FROM AN UNFINISHED POEM.

'Tis noon.   At noon the Hebrew bowed the knee
And worshipped, while the husbandmen withdrew
From the scorched field, and the wayfaring man
Grew faint, and turned aside by bubbling fount,
Or rested in the shadow of the palm.

　　I, too, amid the overflow of day,
Behold the power which wields and cherishes
The frame of Nature.   From this brow of rock
That overlooks the Hudson's western marge,
I gaze upon the long array of groves,
The piles and gulfs of verdure drinking in
The grateful heats.   They love the fiery sun;
Their broadening leaves grow glossier, and their sprays
Climb as he looks upon them.   In the midst,
The swelling river, into his green gulfs,
Unshadowed save by passing sails above,
Takes the redundant glory, and enjoys
The summer in his chilly bed.   Coy flowers
That would not open in the early light,
Push back their plaited sheaths.   The rivulet's pool,
That darkly quivered all the morning long
In the cool shade, now glimmers in the sun;
And o'er its surface shoots, and shoots again,
The glittering dragon-fly, and deep within
Run the brown water-beetles to and fro.

　　A silence, the brief sabbath of an hour,
Reigns o'er the fields; the laborer sits within
His dwelling; he has left his steers awhile,

Unyoked, to bite the herbage, and his dog
Sleeps stretched beside the door-stone in the shade.
Now the grey marmot, with uplifted paws,
No more sits listening by his den, but steals
Abroad, in safety, to the clover-field,
And crops its juicy blossoms. All the while
A ceaseless murmur from the populous town
Swells o'er these solitudes: a mingled sound
Of jarring wheels, and iron hoofs that clash
Upon the stony ways, and hammer-clang,
And creak of engines lifting ponderous bulks,
And calls and cries, and tread of eager feet,
Innumerable, hurrying to and fro.
Noon, in that mighty mart of nations, brings
No pause to toil and care. With early day
Began the tumult, and shall only cease
When midnight, hushing one by one the sounds
Of bustle, gathers the tired brood to rest.

Thus, in this feverish time, when love of gain
And luxury possess the hearts of men,
Thus is it with the noon of human life.
We, in our fervid manhood, in our strength
Of reason, we, with hurry, noise, and care,
Plan, toil, and strive, and pause not to refresh
Our spirits with the calm and beautiful
Of God's harmonious universe, that won
Our youthful wonder; pause not to inquire
Why we are here; and what the reverence
Man owes to man, and what the mystery
That links us to the greater world, beside
Whose borders we but hover for a space.

THE CROWDED STREET.

LET me move slowly through the street,
　　Filled with an ever-shifting train,
Amid the sound of steps that beat
　　The murmuring walks like autumn rain.

How fast the flitting figures come!
　　The mild, the fierce, the stony face;
Some bright with thoughtless smiles, and some
　　Where secret tears have left their trace.

They pass—to toil, to strife, to rest;
　　To halls in which the feast is spread;
To chambers where the funeral guest
　　In silence sits beside the dead.

And some to happy homes repair,
　　Where children, pressing cheek to cheek,
With mute caresses shall declare
　　The tenderness they cannot speak.

And some, who walk in calmness here,
　　Shall shudder as they reach the door
Where one who made their dwelling dear,
　　Its flower, its light, is seen no more.

Youth, with pale cheek and slender frame,
　　And dreams of greatness in thine eye!
Go'st thou to build an early name,
　　Or early in the task to die?

Keen son of trade, with eager brow!
  Who is now fluttering in thy snare?
Thy golden fortunes, tower they now,
  Or melt the glittering spires in air?

Who of this crowd to-night shall tread
  The dance till daylight gleam again?
Who sorrow o'er the untimely dead?
  Who writhe in throes of mortal pain?

Some, famine-struck, shall think how long
  The cold dark hours, how slow the light;
And some, who flaunt amid the throng,
  Shall hide in dens of shame to-night.

Each, where his tasks or pleasures call,
  They pass, and heed each other not.
There is who heeds, who holds them all,
  In his large love and boundless thought.

These struggling tides of life that seem
  In wayward, aimless course to tend,
Are eddies of the mighty stream
  That rolls to its appointed end.

--------•••--------

THE WHITE-FOOTED DEER.

It was a hundred years ago,
  When, by the woodland ways,
The traveller saw the wild deer drink,
  Or crop the birchen sprays.

Beneath a hill, whose rocky side
    O'erbrowed a grassy mead,
And fenced a cottage from the wind,
    A deer was wont to feed.

She only came when on the cliffs
    The evening moonlight lay,
And no man knew the secret haunts
    In which she walked by day.

White were her feet, her forehead showed
    A spot of silvery white,
That seemed to glimmer like a star
    In autumn's hazy night.

And here, when sang the whippoorwill,
    She cropped the sprouting leaves,
And here her rustling steps were heard
    On still October eves.

But when the broad midsummer moon
    Rose o'er that grassy lawn,
Beside the silver-footed deer
    There grazed a spotted fawn.

The cottage dame forbade her son
    To aim the rifle here;
"It were a sin," she said, "to harm
    Or fright that friendly deer.

"This spot has been my pleasant home
    Ten peaceful years and more;
And ever, when the moonlight shines,
    She feeds before our door.

"The red men say that here she walked
　　A thousand moons ago;
They never raise the war-whoop here,
　　And never twang the bow.

"I love to watch her as she feeds,
　　And think that all is well
While such a gentle creature haunts
　　The place in which we dwell."

The youth obeyed, and sought for game
　　In forests far away,
Where, deep in silence and in moss,
　　The ancient woodland lay.

But once, in autumn's golden time,
　　He ranged the wild in vain,
Nor roused the pheasant nor the deer,
　　And wandered home again.

The crescent moon and crimson eve
　　Shone with a mingling light;
The deer, upon the grassy mead,
　　Was feeding full in sight.

He raised the rifle to his eye,
　　And from the cliffs around
A sudden echo, shrill and sharp,
　　Gave back its deadly sound.

Away, into the neighboring wood,
　　The startled creature flew,
And crimson drops at morning lay
　　Amid the glimmering dew.

Next evening shone the waxing moon
  As sweetly as before;
The deer upon the grassy mead
  Was seen again no more.

But ere that crescent moon was old,
  By night the red men came,
And burnt the cottage to the ground,
  And slew the youth and dame.

Now woods have overgrown the mead,
  And hid the cliffs from sight;
There shrieks the hovering hawk at noon,
  And prowls the fox at night.

THE WANING MOON.

I've watched too late; the morn is near;
  One look at God's broad silent sky!
Oh, hopes and wishes vainly dear,
  How in your very strength ye die!

Even while your glow is on the cheek,
  And scarce the high pursuit begun,
The heart grows faint, the hand grows weak,
  The task of life is left undone.

See where, upon the horizon's brim,
  Lies the still cloud in gloomy bars;
The waning moon, all pale and dim,
  Goes up amid the eternal stars.

Late, in a flood of tender light,
  She floated through the ethereal blue,
A softer sun, that shone all night
  Upon the gathering beads of dew.

And still thou wanest, pallid moon!
  The encroaching shadow grows apace;
Heaven's everlasting watchers soon
  Shall see thee blotted from thy place.

Oh, Night's dethroned and crownless queen!
  Well may thy sad, expiring ray
Be shed on those whose eyes have seen
  Hope's glorious visions fade away.

Shine thou for forms that once were bright,
  For sages in the mind's eclipse,
For those whose words were spells of might,
  But falter now on stammering lips!

In thy decaying beam there lies
  Full many a grave on hill and plain,
Of those who closed their dying eyes
  In grief that they had lived in vain.

Another night, and thou among
  The spheres of heaven shalt cease to shine
All rayless in the glittering throng
  Whose lustre late was quenched in thine.

Yet soon a new and tender light
  From out thy darkened orb shall beam,
And broaden till it shines all night
  On glistening dew and glimmering stream.

THE STREAM OF LIFE.

On silvery streamlet of the fields,
  That flowest full and free!
For thee the rains of spring return,
  The summer dews for thee;
And when thy latest blossoms die
  In autumn's chilly showers,
The winter fountains gush for thee,
  Till May brings back the flowers.

Oh Stream of Life! the violet springs
  But once beside thy bed;
But one brief summer, on thy path,
  The dews of heaven are shed.
Thy parent fountains shrink away,
  And close their crystal veins,
And where thy glittering current flowed
  The dust alone remains.

———————•◦•———————

THE UNKNOWN WAY.

A BURNING sky is o'er me,
  The sands beneath me glow,
As onward, onward, wearily,
  In the sultry morn I go.

From the dusty path there opens,
　Eastward, an unknown way;
Above its windings, pleasantly,
　The woodland branches play.

A silvery brook comes stealing
　From the shadow of its trees,
Where slender herbs of the forest stoop
　Before the entering breeze.

Along those pleasant windings
　I would my journey lay,
Where the shade is cool and the dew of night
　Is not yet dried away.

Path of the flowery woodland!
　Oh whither dost thou lead,
Wandering by grassy orchard grounds
　Or by the open mead!

Goest thou by nestling cottage!
　Goest thou by stately hall,
Where the broad elm droops, a leafy dome,
　And woodbines flaunt on the wall!

By steeps where children gather
　Flowers of the yet fresh year!
By lonely walks where lovers stray
　Till the tender stars appear!

Or haply dost thou linger
　On barren plains and bare,
Or clamber the bald mountain side
　Into the thinner air!

Where they who journey upward
  Walk in a weary track,
And oft upon the shady vale
  With longing eyes look back!

I hear a solemn murmur,
  And, listening to the sound,
I knew the voice of the mighty sea,
  Beating his pebbly bound.

Dost thou, oh path of the woodland!
  End where those waters roar,
Like human life, on a trackless beach,
  With a boundless Sea before!

"OH MOTHER OF A MIGHTY RACE."

Oh mother of a mighty race,
Yet lovely in thy youthful grace!
The elder dames, thy haughty peers,
Admire and hate thy blooming years.
    With words of shame
And taunts of scorn they join thy name.

For on thy checks the glow is spread
That tints thy morning hills with red;
They step—the wild deer's rustling feet,
Within thy woods are not more fleet;
    Thy hopeful eye
Is bright as thine own sunny sky.

Aye, let them rail—those haughty ones,
While safe thou dwellest with thy sons.
They do not know how loved thou art,
How many a fond and fearless heart
       Would rise to throw
Its life between thee and the foe.

They know not, in their hate and pride,
What virtues with thy children bide;
How true, how good, thy graceful maids
Make bright, like flowers, the valley shades;
       What generous men
Spring, like thine oaks, by hill and glen.

What cordial welcomes greet the guest
By thy lone rivers of the West;
How faith is kept, and truth revered,
And man is loved, and God is feared,
       In woodland homes,
And where the ocean border foams.

There's freedom at thy gates and rest
For Earth's down-trodden and opprest,
A shelter for the hunted head,
For the starved laborer toil and bread.
       Power, at thy bounds,
Stops and calls back his baffled hounds.

Oh, fair young mother! on thy brow
Shall sit a nobler grace than now.
Deep in the brightness of thy skies,
The thronging years in glory rise,
       And, as they fleet,
Drop strength and riches at thy feet.

Thine eye, with every coming hour,
Shall brighten, and thy form shall tower;
And when thy sisters, elder born,
Would brand thy name with words of scorn,
Before thine eye,
Upon their lips the taunt shall die.

THE LAND OF DREAMS.

A MIGHTY realm is the Land of Dreams,
  With steeps that hang in the twilight sky,
And weltering oceans and trailing streams,
  That gleam where the dusky valleys lie.

But over its shadowy border flow
  Sweet rays from the world of endless morn,
And the nearer mountains catch the glow,
  And flowers in the nearer fields are born.

The souls of the happy dead repair,
  From their bowers of light, to that bordering land,
And walk in the fainter glory there,
  With the souls of the living hand in hand.

One calm sweet smile, in that shadowy sphere,
  From eyes that open on earth no more—
One warning word from a voice once dear—
  How they rise in the memory o'er and o'er!

Far off from those hills that shine with day
  And fields that bloom in the heavenly gales,
The Land of Dreams goes stretching away
  To dimmer mountains and darker vales.

There lie the chambers of guilty delight,
   There walk the spectres of guilty fear,
And soft low voices, that float through the light,
   Are whispering sin in the helpless ear.

Dear maid, in thy girlhood's opening flower,
   Scarce weaned from the love of childish play!
The tears on whose cheeks are but the shower
   That freshens the blooms of early May!

Thine eyes are closed, and over thy brow
   Pass thoughtful shadows and joyous gleams,
And I know, by thy moving lips, that now
   Thy spirit strays in the Land of Dreams.

Light-hearted maiden, oh, heed thy feet!
   O keep where that beam of Paradise falls:
And only wander where thou may'st meet
   The blessed ones from its shining walls.

So shalt thou come from the Land of Dreams,
   With love and peace to this world of strife:
And the light that over that border streams
   Shall lie on the path of thy daily life.

———◆◆◆———

THE BURIAL OF LOVE.

Two dark-eyed maids, at shut of day,
Sat where a river rolled away,
With calm sad brows and raven hair,
And one was pale and both were fair.

Bring flowers, they sang, bring flowers unblown,
Bring forest blooms of name unknown;
Bring budding sprays from wood and wild,
To strew the bier of Love, the child.

Close softly, fondly, while ye weep,
His eyes, that death may seem like sleep,
And fold his hands in sign of rest,
His waxen hands, across his breast.

And make his grave where violets hide,
Where star-flowers strew the rivulet's side,
And blue-birds in the misty spring
Of cloudless skies and summer sing.

Place near him, as ye lay him low,
His idle shafts, his loosened bow,
The silken fillet that around
His waggish eyes in sport he wound.

But we shall mourn him long, and miss
His ready smile, his ready kiss,
The patter of his little feet,
Sweet frowns and stammered phrases sweet;

And graver looks, serene and high,
A light of heaven in that young eye,
All these shall haunt us till the heart
Shall ache and ache—and tears will start.

The bow, the band shall fall to dust,
The shining arrows waste with rust,
And all of Love that earth can claim,
Be but a memory and a name.

Not thus his nobler part shall dwell,
A prisoner in this narrow cell;
But he whom now we hide from men,
In the dark ground, shall live again.

Shall break these clods, a form of light,
With nobler mien and purer sight,
And in the eternal glory stand,
Highest and nearest God's right hand.

THE MAY-SUN SHEDS AN AMBER LIGHT.

The May-sun sheds an amber light
  On new-leaved woods and lawns between;
But she who, with a smile more bright,
  Welcomed and watched the springing green,
      Is in her grave,
      Low in her grave.

The fair white blossoms of the wood
  In groups beside the pathway stand;
But one, the gentle and the good,
  Who cropped them with a fairer hand,
      Is in her grave,
      Low in her grave.

Upon the woodland's morning airs
  The small bird's mingled notes are flung;
But she, whose voice, more sweet than theirs,
  Once bade me listen while they sung,
      Is in her grave,
      Low in her grave.

That music of the early year
  Brings tears of anguish to my eyes;
My heart aches when the flowers appear;
  For then I think of her who lies
             Within her grave,
             Low in her grave.

THE VOICE OF AUTUMN.

THERE comes, from yonder height,
  A soft repining sound,
Where forest leaves are bright,
And fall, like flakes of light,
        To the ground.

It is the autumn breeze,
  That, lightly floating on,
Just skims the weedy leas,
Just stirs the glowing trees,
        And is gone.

He moans by sedgy brook,
  And visits, with a sigh,
The last pale flowers that look,
From out their sunny nook,
        At the sky.

O'er shouting children flies
  That light October wind,
And, kissing cheeks and eyes
He leaves their merry cries
        Far behind.

And wanders on to make
  That soft uneasy sound
By distant wood and lake,
Where distant fountains break
      From the ground.

No bower where maidens dwell
  Can win a moment's stay;
Nor fair untrodden dell;
He sweeps the upland swell,
      And away!

Mourn'st thou thy homeless state?
  Oh soft, repining wind!
That early seek'st and late
The rest it is thy fate
      Not to find.

Not on the mountain's breast,
  Not on the ocean's shore,
In all the East and West:
The wind that stops to rest
      Is no more.

By valleys, woods, and springs,
  No wonder thou shouldst grieve
For all the glorious things
Thou touchest with thy wings
      And must leave.

THE CONQUEROR'S GRAVE.

WITHIN this lowly grave a Conqueror lies,
  And yet the monument proclaims it not,
Nor round the sleeper's name hath chisel wrought
  The emblems of a fame that never dies,
Ivy and amaranth, in a graceful sheaf,
Twined with the laurel's fair, imperial leaf.
     A simple name alone,
     To the great world unknown,
Is graven here, and wild flowers, rising round,
Meek meadow-sweet and violets of the ground,
    Lean lovingly against the humble stone.

Here, in the quiet earth, they laid apart
  No man of iron mould and bloody hands,
Who sought to wreak upon the cowering lands
  The passions that consumed his restless heart;
But one of tender spirit and delicate frame
     Gentlest, in mien and mind,
     Of gentle womankind,
Timidly shrinking from the breath of blame:
One in whose eyes the smile of kindness made
  Its haunt, like flowers by sunny brooks in May,
Yet, at the thought of other's pain, a shade
  Of sweeter sadness chased the smile away.

Nor deem that when the hand that moulders here
Was raised in menace, realms were chilled with fear
  And armies mustered at the sign, as when
Clouds rise on clouds before the rainy East,—
  Gray captains leading bands of veteran men
And fiery youths to be the vulture's feast.

Not thus were waged the mighty wars that gave
The victory to her who fills this grave: .
    Alone her task was wrought,
    Alone the battle fought;
Through that long strife her constant hope was staid
On God alone, nor looked for other aid.

She met the hosts of Sorrow with a look
  That altered not beneath the frown they wore,
And soon the lowering brood were tamed, and took,
  Meekly, her gentle rule, and frowned no more.
Her soft hand put aside the assaults of wrath,
    And calmly broke in twain
    The fiery shafts of pain,
And rent the nets of passion from her path.
  By that victorious hand despair was slain.
With love she vanquished hate and overcame
  Evil with good, in her Great Master's name.

Her glory is not of this shadowy state,
  Glory that with the fleeting season dies;
But when she entered at the sapphire gate
  What joy was radiant in celestial eyes!
How heaven's bright depths with sounding welcomes
    rung,
And flowers of heaven by shining hands were flung
    And He who, long before,
    Pain, scorn, and sorrow bore,
The Mighty Sufferer, with aspect sweet,
Smiled on the timid stranger from his seat;
He who returning, glorious, from the grave,
Dragged Death, disarmed, in chains, a crouching
    slave.

See, as I linger here, the sun grows low;
  Cool airs are murmuring that the night is near
Oh gentle sleeper, from thy grave I go
  Consoled though sad, in hope and yet in fear.
22

Brief is the time, I know,
The warfare scarce begun;
Yet all may win the triumphs thou hast won.
Still flows the fount whose waters strengthened thee;
The victors' names are yet too few to fill
Heaven's mighty roll; the glorious armory,
That ministered to thee, is open still.

NOTES.

Page 13.

POEM OF THE AGES.

In this poem, written and first printed in the year 1821, the author has endeavored, from a survey of the past ages of the world, and of the successive advances of mankind in knowledge, virtue, and happiness, to justify and confirm the hopes of the philanthropist for the future destinies of the human race.

Page 37.

THE BURIAL-PLACE.

The first half of this fragment may seem to the reader borrowed from the essay on Rural Funerals in the fourth number of the Sketch-Book. The lines were, however, written more than a year before that number appeared. The poem, unfinished as it is, would hardly have been admitted into this collection, had not the author been unwilling to lose what had the honor of resembling so beautiful a composition.

Page 43.

THE MASSACRE AT SCIO.

This poem, written about the time of the horrible butchery of the Sciotes by the Turks, in 1824, has been more fortunate than most poetical predictions. The independence of the Greek nation, which it foretold, has come to pass, and the massacre, by inspiring a deeper detestation of their oppressors, did much to promote that event.

Page 43.

Her maiden veil, her own black hair, &c.

"The unmarried females have a modest falling down of the hair over the eyes."—ELIOT.

Page 69.

MONUMENT MOUNTAIN.

The mountain called by this name, is a remarkable precipice in Great Barrington, overlooking the rich and picturesque valley of the Housatonic, in the western part of Massachusetts. At the southern extremity is, or was a few years since, a conical pile of small stones, erected, according to the tradition of the surrounding country, by the Indians, in memory of a woman of the Stockbridge tribe, who killed herself by leaping from the edge of the precipice. Until within few years past, small parties of that tribe used to arrive from their settlement in the western part of the State of New York, on visits to Stockbridge, the place of their nativity and former residence. A young woman belonging to one of these parties, related, to a friend of the author, the story on which the poem of Mountain Monument is founded. An Indian girl had formed an attachment for her cousin, which, according to the customs of the tribe, was unlawful. She was, in consequence, seized with a deep melancholy, and resolved to destroy herself. In company with a female friend, she repaired to the mountain, decked out for the occasion in all her ornaments, and, after passing the day on the summit in singing with her companion the traditional songs of her nation, she threw herself headlong from the rock, and was killed.

Page 80.

THE MURDERED TRAVELLER.

Some years since, in the month of May, the remains of a human body, partly devoured by wild animals, were found in a woody ravine, near a solitary road passing between the mountains west of the village of Stockbridge. It was supposed that the person came to his death by violence, but no traces could be discovered of his murderers. It was only recollected that one evening, in the course of the previous winter, a traveller had stopped at an inn in the village of West Stockbridge; that he had inquired the way to Stockbridge; and that, in paying the innkeeper for something he had ordered, it appeared that he had a considerable sum of money in his possession. Two ill-looking men were present, and went out about the same time that the traveller proceeded on his journey. During the winter, also, two men of shabby appearance, but plentifully supplied with money, had lingered for awhile about the village of Stockbridge. Several years afterward, a criminal, about to be executed for a capital offence in Canada, confessed that he had been concerned in murdering a traveller in Stockbridge for the sake of his money. Nothing was ever discovered respecting the name or residence of the person murdered.

Page 113.

Chained in the market place he stood, &c.

The story of the African Chief, related in this ballad, may be found in the African Repository for April, 1825. The subject of it was a warrior of majestic stature, the brother of Yarradee, king of the Solima nation. He had been taken in battle, and was brought in chains for sale to the Rio Pongas, where he was exhibited in the market-place, his ankles still adorned with the massy rings of gold which he wore when captured. The refusal of his captor to listen to his offers of ransom drove him mad, and he died a maniac.

Page 124.

THE CONJUNCTION OF JUPITER AND VENUS.

This conjunction was said in the common calendars to have taken place on the 2d of August, 1826. This, I believe, was an error, but the apparent approach of the planets was sufficiently near for poetical purposes.

Page 130.

THE HURRICANE.

This poem is nearly a translation from one by José Maria de Heredia, a native of the Island of Cuba, who published at New York, about the year 1825, a volume of poems in the Spanish language.

Page 132.

WILLIAM TELL.

Neither this, nor any of the other sonnets in the collection, with the exception of the one from the Portuguese, is framed according to the legitimate Italian model, which, in the author's opinion, possesses no peculiar beauty for an ear accustomed only to the metrical forms of our own language. The sonnets in this collection are rather poems in fourteen lines than sonnets.

Page 133.

The slim papaya ripens, &c.

Papaya—papaw, custard-apple. Flint, in his excellent work on the Geography and History of the Western States, thus describes this tree and its fruit:

"A papaw shrub, hanging full of fruits, of a size and weight so disproportioned to the stem, and from under long and rich-looking leaves, of the same yellow with the ripened fruit, and of an African luxuriance of growth, is to us one of the richest spectacles that we have ever contemplated in the array of the woods. The fruit contains from two to six seeds like those of the tamarind, except that they are double the size. The pulp of the fruit resembles egg-custard in consistence and appearance. It has the same creamy feeling in the mouth, and unites the taste of eggs, cream, sugar, and spice. It is a natural custard, too luscious for the relish of most people."

Chateaubriand, in his Travels, speaks disparagingly of the fruit of the papaw; but on the authority of Mr. Flint, who must know more of the matter, I have ventured to make my western lover enumerate it among the delicacies of the wilderness.

Page 147.

The surface rolls and fluctuates to the eye.

The prairies of the West, with an undulating surface, *rolling prairies*, as they are called, present to the unaccustomed eye a singular spectacle when the shadows of the clouds are passing rapidly over them. The face of the ground seems to fluctuate and toss like billows of the sea.

Page 147.

The prairie-hawk that, poised on high,
Flaps his broad wings, yet moves not.

I have seen the prairie-hawk balancing himself in the air for hours together, apparently over the same spot; probably watching his prey.

Page 148.

These ample fields
Nourished their harvests.

The size and extent of the mounds in the valley of the Mississippi, indicate the existence, at a remote period, of a nation at once populous and laborious, and therefore probably subsisting by agriculture.

Page 149.

The rude conquerors
Seated the captive with their chiefs.

Instances are not wanting of generosity like this among the North American Indians towards a captive or survivor of a hostile tribe on which the greatest cruelties had been exercised.

Page 150.

SONG OF MARION'S MEN.

The exploits of General Francis Marion, the famous partisan warrior of South Carolina, form an interesting chapter in the annals of the American revolution. The troops were so harassed by the irregular and successful warfare which he kept up at the head of a few daring followers, that they sent an officer to remonstrate with him for not coming into the open field and fighting "like a gentleman and a Christian."

Page 157.

MARY MAGDALEN.

Several learned divines, with much appearance of reason, in particular Dr. Lardner, have maintained that the common notion respecting the dissolute life of Mary Magdalen is erroneous, and that she was always a person of excellent character. Charles Taylor, the editor of Calmet's Dictionary of the Bible, takes the same view of the subject.

The verses of the Spanish poet here translated refer to the "woman who had been a sinner," mentioned in the seventh chapter of St. Luke's Gospel, and who is commonly confounded with Mary Magdalen.

Page 159.

FATIMA AND RADUAN.

This and the following poems belong to that class of ancient Spanish ballads, by unknown authors, called *Romances Moriscos* —Moriscan romances or ballads. They were composed in the 14th century, some of them, probably, by the Moors, who then lived intermingled with the Christians; and they relate the loves and achievements of the knights of Grenada.

Page 161.

LOVE AND FOLLY.—(FROM LA FONTAINE.)

This is rather an imitation than a translation of the poem of the graceful French fabulist.

Page 165.

These eyes shall not recall thee, &c.

This is the very expression of the original—*No te llamarán mis ojos, &c.* The Spanish poets early adopted the practice of calling a lady by the name of the most expressive feature of her countenance, her eyes. The lover styled his mistress "ojos bellos," beautiful eyes; "ojos serenos," serene eyes. Green eyes seem to have been anciently thought a great beauty in Spain, and there is a very pretty ballad by an absent lover, in which he addressed his lady by the title of "green eyes;" supplicating that he may remain in her remembrance.

> ¡Ay ojuelos verdes!
> Ay los mis ojuelos!
> Ay, hagan los cielos
> Que de mi te acuerdes!

Page 167.

Say, Love—for thou didst see her tears, &c.

The stanza beginning with this line stands thus in the original :—

> Dilo tu, amor, si lo viste;
> ¡Mas ay! que de lastimado
> Diste otro nudo á la venda,
> Para no ver lo que ha pasado.

I am sorry to find so poor a conceit deforming so spirited a composition as this old ballad, but I have preserved it in the version. It is one of those extravagances which afterwards became so common in Spanish poetry, when Gongora introduced the *estilo culto*, as it was called.

Page 168.

LOVE IN THE AGE OF CHIVALRY.

This personification of the passion of Love, by Peyro Vidal, has been referred to as a proof of how little the Provençal poets were indebted to the authors of Greece and Rome for the imagery of their poems.

Page 169.

THE LOVE OF GOD.—(FROM THE PROVENÇAL OF BERNARD RASCAS.)

The original of these lines is thus given by John of Nostradamus, in his lives of the Troubadours, in a barbarous Frenchified orthography :—

> Tonta kansa mortala una fes perira,
> Fors que l'amour de Dieu, que touslours durara.
> Tous nostres cors vendran essachs, como fa l'eska,
> Lous Aubres leyssaran lour verdour tendra o fresca,
> Lous Ausselets del bosc perdran lour kant subtyeu,
> E non s'auzira plus lou Rossignol gentyeu.
> Lous Buols al Pastourgage, e las blankas fedettas
> Sent'ran lous agulhons de las mortals Sagettas,
> Lous crestas d'Arles fiers, Renards, o Loups espars
> Kabrols, Cervys, Chamous, Senglars de toutes pars,
> Lous Ours hardys e forts, seran poudra, o Arena,

Lou Daulphin en la Mar, lou Ton, e la Balena,
Monstres impetuous, Ryaumes, e Comtas,
Lous Princes, e lous Reys, seran per mort domtas,
E nota ben eysso káscun : la Terra granda,
(Ou l'Escritura ment) lou fermament que branda,
Prendra autra figura. Enfin tout perira,
Fors que l'Amour de Dieu, que touiours durará.

Page 170.

Las Auroras de Diana, in which the original of these lines
is contained, is, notwithstanding it was praised by Lope do Vega,
one of the worst of the old Spanish Romances, being a tissue of
riddles and affectations, with now and then a little poem of considerable beauty.

Page 184.

EARTH.

The author began this poem in rhyme. The following is the
first draught of it as far as he proceeded, in a stanza which he
found it convenient to abandon.

A midnight black with clouds is on the sky ;
  A shadow like the first original night
Folds in, and seems to press me as I lie ;
  No image meets the vainly wandering sight,
And shot through rolling mists no starlight gleam
Glances on glassy pool or rippling stream.

No ruddy blaze, from dwellings bright within,
  Tinges the flowering summits of the grass ;
No sound of life is heard, no village din,
  Wings rustling overhead or steps that pass,
While, on the breast of earth at random thrown,
I listen to her mighty voice alone.

A voice of many tones ; deep murmurs sent
  From waters that in darkness glide away,
From woods unseen by sweeping breezes bent,
  From rocky chasms where darkness dwells all day,
And hollows of the invisible hills around,
Blent in one ceaseless, melancholy sound.

Oh Earth ! dost thou, too, sorrow for the past ?
  Mourn'st thou thy childhood's unreturning hours,
Thy springs, that briefly bloomed and faded fast,
  The gentle generations of thy flowers,
Thy forests of the elder time, decayed
And gone with all the tribes that loved their shade ?

Mourn'st thou that first fair time so early lost,
   The golden age that lives in poets' strains,
Ere hail or lightning, whirlwind, flood or frost
   Scathed thy green breast, or earthquakes whelmed thy plains!
Ere blood upon the shuddering ground was spilt,
Or night was haunted by disease and guilt?

Or haply dost thou grieve for those who die?
   For living things that trod awhile thy face,
The love of thee and heaven, and now they lie
   Mixed with the shapeless dust the wild winds chase?
I, too, must grieve, for never on thy sphere
Shall those bright forms and faces reappear.

Ha! with a deeper and more thrilling tone,
   Rises that voice around me, 'tis the cry
Of Earth for guilt and wrong, the eternal moan
   Sent to the listening and long-suffering sky.
I hear and tremble, and my heart grows faint,
As midst the night goes up that great complaint.

Page 199.

Where Isar's clay-white rivulets run
Through the dark woods, like frighted deer.

Close to the city of Munich, in Bavaria, lies the spacious and beautiful pleasure-ground, called the English Garden, in which these lines were written, originally projected and laid out by our countryman, Count Rumford, under the auspices of one of the sovereigns of the country. Winding walks of great extent, pass through close thickets and groves interspersed with lawns; and streams, diverted from the river Isar, traverse the grounds swiftly in various directions, the water of which, stained with the clay of the soil it has corroded in its descent from the upper country, is frequently of a turbid white color.

Page 204.

THE GREEN MOUNTAIN BOYS.

This song refers to the expedition of the Vermonters, commanded by Ethan Allen, by whom the British fort of Ticonderoga, on Lake Champlain, was surprised and taken, in May, 1775.

Page 206.

THE CHILD'S FUNERAL.

The incident on which this poem is founded was related to the author while in Europe, in a letter from an English lady. A child died in the south of Italy, and when they went to bury it they found it revived and playing with the flowers which, after the manner of that country, had been brought to grace its funeral.

Page 211.

'Tis said, when Schiller's death drew nigh,
The wish possessed his mighty mind,
To wander forth wherever lie
The homes and haunts of human kind.

Shortly before the death of Schiller, he was seized with a strong desire to travel in foreign countries, as if his spirit had a presentiment of its approaching enlargement, and already longed to expatiate in a wider and more varied sphere of existence.

Page 213.

The flower
Of Sanguinaria, from whose brittle stem
The red drops fell like blood.

The *Sanguinaria Canadensis*, or blood-root, as it is commonly called, bears a delicate white flower of a musky scent, the stem of which breaks easily, and distils a juice of a bright red color.

Page 219.

The shad-bush, white with flowers,
Brightened the glens.

The small tree, named by the botanists *Aronia Botyrapium*, is called, in some parts of our country, the shad-bush, from the circumstance that it flowers about the time that the shad ascend the rivers in early spring. Its delicate sprays, covered with white blossoms before the trees are yet in leaf, have a singularly beautiful appearance in the woods.

Page 220.

" There hast thou," said my friend, " a fitting type
Of human life.

I remember hearing an aged man, in the country, compare the slow movement of time in early life and its swift flight as it approaches old age, to the drumming of a partridge or ruffed grouse in the woods—the strokes falling slow and distinct at first, and following each other more and more rapidly, till they end at last in a whirring sound.

Page 222.

AN EVENING REVERY.—FROM AN UNFINISHED POEM.

This poem and that entitled the Fountain, with one or two others in blank verse, were intended by the author as portions of a larger poem, in which they may hereafter take their place.

Page 224.

The fresh savannas of the Sangamon
Here rise in gentle swells, and the long grass
Is mixed with rustling hazels.   Scarlet tufts
Are glowing in the green, like flakes of fire.

The Painted Cup, *Euchroma Coccinea*, or *Bartsia Coccinea*, grows in great abundance in the hazel prairies of the western states, where its scarlet tufts make a brilliant appearance in the midst of the verdure.   The Sangamon is a beautiful river, tributary to the Illinois, bordered with rich prairies.

Page 233.

The long wave rolling from the southern pole
To break upon Japan.

"Breaks the long wave that at the pole began."—TENNENT'S ANSTER FAIR.

Page 234.

At noon the Hebrew bowed the knee
And worshipped.

"Evening and morning, and at noon, will I pray and cry aloud, and he shall hear my voice."—PSALM lv. 17.

Page 237.

THE WHITE-FOOTED DEER.

"During the stay of Long's Expedition at Engineer Cantonment, three specimens of a variety of the common deer were brought in, having all the feet white near the hoofs, and extending to those on the hind feet from a little above the spurious hoofs.   This white extremity was divided, upon the sides of the foot, by the general color of the leg, which extends down near to the hoofs, leaving a white triangle in front, of which the point was elevated rather higher than the spurious hoofs."—GODMAN'S NATURAL HISTORY, vol. ii. p. 314.